The Selected Works of Mahasweta Devi

Mahasweta Devi (1926–2016) was one of India's foremost literary personalities, a prolific and best-selling author in Bengali of short fiction and novels; a deeply political social activist who worked with and for indigenous and marginalized communities like the landless labourers of eastern India for years; the editor of a quarterly, *Bortika*, in which marginalized peoples themselves documented grassroot-level issues and trends; and a socio-political commentator whose articles appeared regularly in the *Economic and Political Weekly*, *Frontier* and other journals.

Mahasweta Devi made important contributions to literary and cultural studies in this country. Her empirical research into oral history as it lives in the cultures and memories of tribal communities was a first of its kind. Her powerful, haunting tales of exploitation and struggle have been seen as rich sites of feminist discourse by leading scholars. Her innovative use of language expanded the conventional borders of Bengali literary expression. Standing at the intersection of vital contemporary questions of politics, gender and class, she was a significant figure in the field of socially committed literature.

Recognizing this, we have conceived a publishing programme which encompasses a representational look at the complete Mahasweta: her novels, her short fiction, her children's stories, her plays, her activist prose writings. The series is an attempt to introduce her impressive body of work to a readership beyond Bengal; it is also an overdue recognition of the importance of her contribution to the literary and cultural history of our country.

T0332351

MOTHER OF 1084

MAHASWETA DEVI

Translated with an introductory essay by
SAMIK BANDYOPADHYAY

LONDON NEW YORK CALCUTTA

First printing 1997
Second printing 1998
Third printing 2001
Fourth printing 2007
Fifth printing 2008
Sixth printing 2011
Seventh printing 2014
Eighth printing 2016
Ninth printing 2018
Tenth printing 2019
Eleventh printing 2021

Seagull Books, 2019

ISBN 978 8 1 7046 139 5

British Library Cataloguing-in-Publication Data
A catalogue record for this book is available from the British Library

Typeset by Seagull Books, Calcutta, India
Printed and bound by Hyam Enterprises, Calcutta, India

CONTENTS

Introduction

SAMIK BANDYOPADHYAY

When Mahasweta Devi (b. 14 January 1926) wrote the first version of *Hajar Churashir Ma* (*Mother of 1084*) in September 1973 for the October issue of the periodical *Prasad*, following it up with a considerably revised and enlarged version for its publication as a book in early 1974, the more visible and widespread phase of the Naxalite movement was already over (though it has survived with its militancy intact in some pockets, mostly in a few districts in the south, with the media reporting from time to time 'encounters' or clashes that leave several dead—armymen, policemen, landlords and their toadies, and of course the Naxalites themselves), the result of repression taking its toll, and scaring away the more faddist section of the urban student radicals who had joined the movement, but were soon running for their lives and cushy positions, and exposing the movement in the ultimate act of betrayal. In the daylong enlightenment two years after the dastardly killing of her son, Brati, that Sujata, mother of corpse number 1084, has to undergo to find a moral rationale for her son's rebellion, the two central chapters are devoted to repression and betrayal.

At the same time, as Mahasweta explains, 'Sujata, in *Mother of 1084*, is essentially apolitical. Yet as she reaches towards an explanation of the death of her son killed in the 70s, she too finds the entire social system cadaverous, and as she takes a closer look at the society, she finds no legitimacy for his death.' It is an illegitimacy that Mahasweta locates spread throughout society, in the administration, in the cultural–intellectual establishment, in politics, in the existence of a whole antisocial fringe of killers prepared to serve the interests of any organized political force anywhere between the extremes of the Right and those of the Left. In a narrative style that allows simultaneously for an evocation of the illegitimacy rampant at all these levels as more than a setting and a focusing on an individual's independent realization, Mahasweta begins with the exposure of the morality of a family, takes Sujata out of its confines to let her meet and interact with others lying beyond, only to bring her back to the family at the end, and then let her make a last, desperate effort to accept its norms and adjust to it, before she collapses. The end is ambiguous, but becomes significant, thanks to the thin line of a clue that Mahasweta keeps running from the beginning—the pain of appendicitis and the painkiller tablets. For while it allows Dibyanath to rationalize and put a lid on the facts—'The appendix has burst': the gross physicalization that a gross physical man like Dibyanath would naturally make—the collapse is the natural culmination of a spiritual (a word one is compelled to use in the absence of anything better to convey an inextricably intimate commingling of the rational and the emotional) struggle, learning to understand for the first time, and knowing at the end of it that there is no forgiveness after such knowledge. The sharply contradictory perceptions confronting each other from time to time, only to be shoved underground almost immediately, come to a head at this point, as Sujata faces the Dibyanath–Saroj Pal nexus—corrupt power/authority in state/society in its affiliation with corrupt power/ authority in family in evidence in dramatic terms.

Saroj Pal, the mastermind behind the annihilation of Brati and his comrades, makes his appearance as a very special guest at a family function—an engagement party for the dead Brati's sister, on Brati's birthday, coincidentally the day of his death too; this is made all the more dramatic, when Saroj Pal cannot come in, since he is 'on duty', and Sujata has to receive him; and the dramatic encounter between the two—'the black car' and the words 'on duty' conjure up a rush of associations, drawing the whole day's experiences and recalled memories together with explosive force: 'Duty still? Still in uniform? The black car, the bullet-proof chain armour underneath the shirt, the pistol in the holster, the helmeted sentry in the rear seat? Where's the unquiet? Where's the duty?' It was Nandini, who had told her—screamed—that 'nothing has quietened down, it can't . . . Don't say that it has all cooled down.' For Sujata, 'the black car' and the word 'duty' confirm the information that Nandini had screamed out to her, convey both a promise/hope and a threat, the hope of redemption of accumulated injustice and the threat of state violence in the defence of vested interests; and it is the shock of that insight into potential history—more than anything physical—that drives Sujata to that final 'long-drawn-out, heartrending, poignant cry'.

It is part of Mahasweta's narrative method to rise from time to time from the clinical/documentary accumulation of facts in objective sequence to a passionate lyrical lift, as in this particular case; the cry no longer a mere cry, but a charged gesture of 'blood, protest, grief' (Mahasweta's words are 'smelt of', conveying the charge in even more sensuous terms) that tears away from—even as it tears down—the neatly structured grid of time, defined so elaborately in so many different ways, from the series of references to dates and specific moments in time, and the most precise accounting for time lags/intervals and time sequences in the first few pages ('a morning twenty-two years ago'; 'the pain had come at eight in the evening'; 'Jyoti was ten at the time, Neepa eight, Tuli six'; 'then the dawn of seventeenth January and Brati was born. It was the morning of seventeenth January again'; 'Sujata turned fifty-one two years ago, Jyoti's father turned fifty-six'; 'Two years ago, early on the seventeenth of January, on Brati's birthday, on the very day that had brought Brati to the world, the news on the telephone had burst upon the neat and clean household and the nice, calm family with a violence that did not fit into any pattern') and of course the time locus of the chapters which are set in the morning, the afternoon, the late afternoon and the evening respectively. Mahasweta's flight from time to timelessness, or a point in time extended to future history, is a narrative device growing out of an attitude that may be related to Gramsci's favourite motto (as he puts it in his letter from prison to Tatiana, dated 6 November 1932): 'pessimism of the intelligence, optimism of the will'.

In her narrative, Mahasweta does not give any historical account of the Naxalite movement in West Bengal, that broke out in the tribal region of Naxalbari in northern West Bengal, in May 1967, when a policeman, Sonam Wangdi, was killed by armed tribals resisting a police combing of the village for one of their underground leaders, and the police force, in retaliation, fired upon the villagers, killing nine, including six women and two children. The regional movement grew and spread fast, drawing in a wide assortment of elements, including a considerable section of urban students; but with inadequate organizational control and sharp differences in the leadership over both ideological and strategic issues, mounting persecution, and, above all else, the Left establishment's use of state machinery both to disinform the people and the ranks alike and to drive power to the extreme of brutality, the movement collapsed in 1971. In later works, Mahasweta would explore the politics and the passions of the peasant–tribal revolt (against a State power wielded, in the state, by a United Front led by Communists) turning into a students' revolt against bourgeois values and the academic institutions they sustained. She has a more limited objective in *Mother of 1084*:

> In the 70s, in the Naxalite movement, I saw exemplary integrity, selflessness and the guts to die for a cause. I thought I saw history in the making, and decided that as a writer it would be my mission to document it. As a writer, I feel a commitment to my times, to mankind and to myself. I did not consider the Naxalite movement an isolated happening . . . In the Naxalite movement I saw only a further extension of the movements of the past, especially the Tebhaga, Kakdwip and Telengana uprisings. In my work *Agnigarbha* (The Fire Within, 1978), located in the rural experience, I produced a work far more important than my *Hajar Churashir Ma*. In the latter I portrayed the

Naxalite movement in its urban phase in 1971–74; and against that and a generation gap, I set an apolitical mother's quest to know her martyred Naxalite son, to know what he stood for; for she had not known the true Brati ever, as long as he had been alive. Death brings him closer to her through her quest.

In the same note on her writing from which I translated the lines immediately preceding, Mahasweta insists, 'I believe in the value of documentation.' As far as documentation goes, her account of the state of the movement in its last urban phase touches on almost all its features, as they are recorded by Sumanta Banerjee in his authoritative history of the movement, *In the Wake of Naxalbari* (Calcutta 1980, *The Simmering Revolution*, in its London edition):

> With increasing help from the Centre and imported paramilitary and military forces, police retaliation against the CPI(M-L) urban guerrillas began to gain momentum from the last quarter of 1970. No mercy was shown to any CPI(M-L) cadre or supporter if caught . . . As the New Year 1971 began, the approach of another mid-term poll cast an ominous shadow over West Bengal. The old rivalry between the CPI(M) and CPI(M-L) cadres had already appeared in a much more virulent form. Leaders of both parties reared up their ranks on mutual suspicion and hostility . . . Clashes between the ranks of the two parties increased . . . Soon certain localities in Calcutta and its suburbs came to be demarcated by the two parties, each carving out its own sphere of

influence. Trespass by any party man in areas dominated by the rival party was punished with death. A bloody cycle of interminable assaults and counter-assaults, murders and vendetta, was initiated. The ranks of both the CPI(M) and CPI(M-L) dissipated their militancy in mutual fightings leading to the elimination of a large number of their activists, and leaving the field open to the police and the hoodlums. It was a senseless orgy of murders, misplaced fury, sadistic tortures, acted out with the vicious norms of the underworld, and dictated by the decadent and cunning values of the petty bourgeois leaders . . . The lumpen proletariat were put to use in two ways. Some were used as agent-provocateurs, who precipitated some violent action and exposed the unwarned CPI(M-L) cadres in a locality to an unanticipated police raid. It was a sort of 'corpus delicti' which provided the police with an opportunity to pick up whom they wanted. Some other members of the lumpen proletariat were bought over . . . and set upon the CPI(M-L) leaders and cadres. In official parlance their actions came to be known as 'people's resistance to Naxalite depredations' . . .

Readers of *Mother of 1084* will find in Banerjee's analysis the politics that lay behind the brutal massacre of Brati and his comrades: the lumpen proletariat killers who constitute a local mafia and a standing threat to survivors like Somu's mother and sister, or traitors like Anindya, who 'had come with definite instructions' from the parent party to penetrate the ranks of the dissidents 'as part of a political manoeuvre' to betray them to the police. Banerjee does not wish away the violence perpetrated by the urban guerrillas, and even finds the inevitable connection between the red terror and the white. Mahasweta has her own logic in her identification with the apolitical mother in keeping out the Naxalite violence. The mother would naturally see only the victim in her son.

She, however, has an additional justification inherent in the timing of Sujata's quest and that of the killing itself, for the references to the Barasat killing in November 1970, when the bodies of eleven young men with their hands tied behind them, were found slaughtered on the road to Barasat, and the Baranagar killing on 12 August 1971, when more than a hundred Naxalites were hounded out from their dens and decapitated in broad daylight, make the killing of Brati and his comrades part of the organized massacre of the Naxalites in 1970–71, perpetrated by the police, the party in power, hired goons, and even parties of the Left establishment acting in unholy collusion; a phase when the urban Naxalites were in utter disarray and retreat, and were entirely at the receiving end.

In *Mother of 1084* even while Mahasweta evokes and re-creates the killings of the Naxalites, she concentrates on the later reactions—and lack of reaction—of a cross section of the survivors, both those who bear the scars and wounds—both literally and figuratively—of those horrible days and those who had lived through the days of violence in simulated insularity. The adoration of godmen, the euphoria over the Bangladesh war, the fashionable pretences of literary radicalism, and scandals, commercial and amorous, constituted for the latter a lifestyle that guaranteed their security. What stands out in Mahasweta's elaborate exposure of the Chatterjee family and its art of survival is their systematic denial of Brati and his defiance of the family—beginning with Dibyanath's active concern to keep the news of the manner of Brati's killing 'from the people who knew him': 'Dibyanath had not allowed Sujata to take his car. It would not be the right thing to keep his car waiting before Kantapukur. Anybody could identify the car . . . Dibyanath had succeeded in his mission, his string-pulling. The next day the newspapers reported the deaths of four young men. Their names were reported. Brati was not mentioned in any of the reports.'

At one level at least, the urban guerrillas were reacting against the immorality of this lifestyle that celebrated and cultivated survival at any cost, and rejecting the social familial system that had nurtured them. Objective studies of the Naxalite movement (including Sumanta Banerjee's, cited earlier) would not accept this as a major motivation for the majority of urban guerrillas; but as far as Mahasweta is concerned, that would be the one aspect that could rationalize the movement and Brati's death to a fairly affluent, sensitive and enlightened mother, who had read in   her son's special concern for her his understanding of her daily humiliation as a woman and her quiet, determined struggle for self-assertion and independence, which ironically gathers force and momentum from Brati's death.

In *Mother of 1084*, Mahasweta attempts a variation of her narrative style more characteristically evident in her historical novels, in the same effort to make the particular situation not paradigmatic (for that could amount to simplification), but to locate it at the hub of a more complex situation or chain of developments in history. There are three homes, representing three different cultures/

locations/economies in *Mother of 1084*—Sujata's, Somu's mother's and Nandini's. It goes to the credit of Mahasweta's penchant for realism that she is able to convey, with the utmost precision and economy of detail, the family structures and their economic implications as they go to define the individualities of the three women to the point of setting up a hierarchy of self-assertion/independence: from Somu's mother at the lowest rung to Nandini at the highest, with Sujata at an intermediate level. There are hints/traces of mobility between the rungs, with indications of possibilities. The helpless fear and submission of Somu's mother (voiced in her pleadingly insistent 'didis', literally 'elder sister', interspersed through her address) has a foil in the resentment/anger of Somu's sister, who is also a foil to Sujata, offering a more inchoate version of Sujata's own dogged resistance to the power imposed on her by Dibyanath and family (both independent earners, though the circumstances that have motivated them to the choice have been so different). Nandini is the one who *knows*, and has *decided*, while Sujata is in the throes of learning/knowing, and edging towards deciding. In fact, it is only on her return from her daylong odyssey that Sujata confronts/challenges Dibyanath for the first time—a step up the hierarchic ladder—'Her words hit him like a whiplash. Dibyanath went out tamely, wiping the nape of his neck.' There is also the suggestion that it is Nandini's political/ideological commitment and analytic understanding that give her the strength to endure and carry on. It is Nandini who explains and clarifies the issues of rebellion, power, betrayal and also revolutionary optimism.

Sujata's meeting with Nandini is not only the last in the series and the most illuminating, but there is a neat spatial logic in the route followed for the quest: with the colony where Somu's mother lived in the 'ramshackle house, with moss on the roof, cracked walls patched up with cardboard', at the farthest end from Sujata's locus, both topographically and socially, and Nandini's place, 'quite close to her own', 'an old-fashioned two-storeyed building, with a verandah running in front'. Obviously, it has been a journey away and back, with understanding growing in the process, and naturally drawing more from Nandini, a neighbour, socially, culturally and topographically. The distinction between Somu's mother and Nandini is underscored in terms of the different histories of their homes: Nandini's home, once owned by rich ancestors, the family split up in the later generations and split into sectors of wealth and poverty; and Somu's mother's, part of the 'first of the colonies in West Bengal where the residents had grabbed the land and settled down'. Sujata's sense of insecurity and precariousness in Somu's mother's house is in contrast to the assurance that is hers in Nandini's, in spite of Nandini's severer tone. She makes up her mind at Nandini's place: 'Sujata would not live in this house after tonight.' While Nandini's determination must have been a factor in her being able to decide, what is more important in the narrative design is the fact of rejection that she faces from both, leaving her entirely on her own. The process of understanding has ended with a compulsion to decide.

One fails to see how Gayatri Chakravorty Spivak can find *Mother of 1084* written in a prose that 'belonged to the generally sentimental style of the mainstream Bengali novel of the fifties and sixties' (*In Other Worlds*, New York, 1987). Between the mid-40s and 60s, mainstream Bengali fiction gained a tightening and a sharpening, and in the hands of the three great Bandyopadhyays—Tarashankar, Bibhutibhushan and Manik—and then with Premendra Mitra, Narendranath Mitra, Subodh Ghosh and Samaresh Bose, the sentimental streak had given way to a harder and colder style. This is the prose that Mahasweta inherits and loosens and enriches with voices from the street, the fields and the forest—in *Mother of 1084* in particular, the language of the graffiti on the city walls, the political slogans— in sharp and ironic contrast to the language of 'the fashionable set'. Mahasweta's prose has all along offered these juxtapositions and clashes, 'voicing' in the process the tensions and confrontations in the society that she chooses as her space. The narratorial voice in *Mother of 1084* submits to Sujata's emerging voice which in its turn rises above the voices at the party. At one level, the work is all about a woman finding a voice of her own, distinctive from all the other voices she has negotiated with, including those of her family, Saroj Pal, Somu's mother, Nandini, Brati when alive, Hem and those at the party. In the first chapter, the evocation of Saroj Pal is through the clipped, authoritarian voice, first over the telephone (an important object in its own right in the narrative), and then directly, but almost exclusively as the disembodied, brutal voice of power. There is the completion of a circuit when Sujata, once silenced by the voice of Saroj Pal—the series of No's ('No, your son didn't go to Digha', 'No, we won't let you keep these', 'No, you won't get the pictures')—recalled significantly at this point, with associated images—'the brass badge of authority', 'the aluminium door bearing the slogan—No Mercy for Saroj Pal'—finds her voice in the cry that sets 'oblivion itself, the present and the future atremble, reeling under its impact'. One has to identify and distinguish the different voices with their class cultural indices being defined in the dialogue units against the narratorial voice to read the drama of internal change/charge and rebellion growing in the process to the final point of eruption/explosion.

There has been an attempt in the translation to capture the voices, and I have enjoyed the rare privilege of the author's active participation in the work. In fact, at one stage Mahasweta Devi had done a rough translation of a little over one-third of the novel, adding quite a few new slants for incorporation in my version, and handed it over to me for any use I would like to make of it. The translation has grown through at least three drafts, and been laid aside for long spells for a really fresh look and consequent revision, all aimed at a dependable translation.

Morning

In her dreams Sujata was back on a morning twenty-two years ago. She often went back to that morning. She found herself packing her bag: towel, blouse, sari, toothbrush, soap. Sujata is fifty-three now. In her dreams she sees a Sujata at thirty-one, busy packing her bag. A Sujata still young, heavy with the child she bore in her womb, packed her bag carefully, item by item, as she prepared to bring Brati into this world. That Sujata's face twisted with pain again and again, she clamped her teeth on her lips to check the cry, the Sujata of the dreams waiting for Brati to be born.

The pain had come at eight in the evening. Hem with all her experience had said, It won't take time, Ma. The womb has started pushing it out. Hem had held her hands and said, Let all be well. Let God bring you back, the two of you separate.

There was pain, a terrible pain. Sujata was in the nursing home from the day before, for she had been warned that the child could come any moment. Jyoti was ten at the time, Neepa eight, Tuli six. Her mother-in-law had waited with her, she remembered. Jyoti's father was the only child of his mother. She had lost her husband after her first son. She could not stand Sujata having her children, she looked at her with withering hatred. When the time for childbirth approached, she would leave the house to go and live with her sister. She refused to stand by Sujata.

Her husband said, Ma is too soft, can't you understand that? She can't stand all this pain and the commotion.

But Sujata never cried out, she did not even groan. She pressed her teeth tight on her lips and did all that she had to do for her children. That was the one time that her mother-in-law was with them, because her sister had gone out of Calcutta. Sujata's husband was then in Kanpur on business. Dibyanath had not known that his mother would stay on this time. She never stayed at such times, she would not this time either, that was what he had thought. Still he had not made any arrangements for Sujata. He never did. The first pain came in the bathroom, and Sujata trembled all over. The sight of blood frightened her. She packed up all her things herself, and asked the cook to call a taxi.

She went to the nursing home all by herself. The doctor looked concerned. She was scared. As the pains came, Sujata's eyes seemed to grope in a haze; somebody seemed to be holding a smoked glass before her eyes. With an effort she opened her eyes wide and asked the doctor,

Am I all right?

Of course.

Child?

Go to sleep.

What will you do?

An operation.

Doctor, child?

Go to sleep, I'm here to take care of everything.

Why did you come by yourself?

My husband's out of town.

Sujata was surprised. She had not expected her husband to come with her even if he had been in town. Why should the doctor expect it? Dibyanath never came with her, never accompanied her when it was time. He slept in a room on the second floor lest the cries of the newborn disturbed his sleep. He would never come down to ask about the children when they were ill. But he noticed things, he noticed Sujata, he had to be sure that Sujata was fit enough to bear a child again.

Are you taking your tonic regularly?

Dibyanath's voice sounded deep and phlegmy. When a restless lust stirred him, Dibyanath's throat seemed to secrete phlegm till his voice laboured under a viscous load. Sujata knew Dibyanath only too well. When Dibyanath showed concern about her health, it could have only one meaning. How could the doctor know anything about Dibyanath?

The doctor prescribed a medicine for Sujata. But the pain persisted. Suddenly Sujata felt a burning desire for the child. Six years had passed after the birth of Tuli. Sujata had defended herself determinedly but had failed in the end.

She had felt herself violated and defiled throughout the nine months. The body gathering weight seemed a curse. But the moment she realized that her life and the child's was in danger, she felt a surge of compassion. Sujata had at once called for the doctor. She had asked him, Please operate. Save the child.

That's what we're going to do.

The nurse gave an injection. The pain pierced Sujata's stomach through and through. Nineteen forty-eight. Sixteenth January. Sujata's hands gripped and crumpled the white bedsheet again and again. Her forehead gleamed with perspiration. The black mark under the eye stretched, grew bigger. Sujata did not feel the winter's cold. It was a bitterly cold January that year.

The pain pierced her stomach through and through. Sujata woke up dripping with sweat, her hands clutching the white bedsheet. When she saw her husband in the bed beside her, her long brows twitched into a frown. Why should her husband be in the bed next to hers? She shook her head. The day Brati was born Jyoti's father was nowhere near, hence he never appeared in her dreams. But Sujata was dreaming no longer.

She stretched out her hand. Baralgan tablet. Water. She took the tablet, drank a sip of water. Wiped her forehead with the end of her sari.

Then she lay down again. She had to count from one to hundred. That was what the doctor had instructed. As she counted, the pain subsided. In the time that it took, the Baralgan began to work. The pain abated.

The pain subsided. It left Sujata exhausted, overcome. The pain had to subside. She looked at the clock. It was six in the morning. She looked at the wall. The calendar. Seventeenth January. The whole of the night of the other sixteenth of January she had had the pain tearing through her, from consciousness to unconsciousness and back again, the smell of ether, harsh lights, the doctors moving beyond the hazy screen of torpid pain, all night long, all night long, then the dawn of seventeenth January and Brati was born. It was the morning of seventeenth January again. But there lay back in the past, two years ago, yet another seventeenth of January, yet another dawn, when Sujata slept beside the same man in the same manner. And the telephone rang. On the bedside table. Suddenly.

The telephone rang this morning too. From Jyoti's room. Jyoti had removed it to his room soon after that day two years ago. So, so considerate Jyoti. Her first son, her eldest. Dibyanath's loyal and obedient son. Bini's generous husband. Suman's loving father.

Sujata turned fifty-one two years ago, Jyoti's father turned fifty-six. The safest years in life. Everything seemed settled, organized. The eldest daughter was married already, the younger daughter had made her choice. The eldest son was established in his career, the father had plans to send the younger son abroad for further studies. Everything seemed so well organized, orderly, neat and beautiful.

And it was right then that the telephone rang. Sujata had lifted the receiver in a half-awakened daze. An unknown, impersonal officer's voice had asked the first question—Are you related to Brati Chatterjee?

Your son, you say? Come to Kantapukur.

Yes, the faceless, disembodied voice had repeated, Come to Kantapukur. The receiver had crashed to the floor, Sujata had fainted.

Two years ago, early on the seventeenth of January, on Brati's birthday, on the very day that had brought Brati to the world, the news on the telephone had burst upon the neat and clean household and the nice, calm family with a violence that did not fit into any pattern.

That was why Jyoti had removed the telephone from its place soon after. Sujata came to know of it later. For three months she knew nothing. She lay in her bed all the time, with her eyes shrouded by her hands. She never cried aloud. Hem alone stayed with her to give her sleeping pills or hold her hands.

Sujata did not know when the telephone was removed from the room.

It took Sujata three months to start going to her job at the bank again. She again spoke normally to Jyoti, Neepa and Tuli. She again sharpened the pencil for Suman, Jyoti's son. She asked Jyoti's wife, Bini, Did you send my black-bordered sari to be washed?

When Jyoti's father went to Bombay, she put his digestives for him into the suitcase.

Only when everything was normal again did Sujata notice that the telephone had been removed from her room to Jyoti's.

When she first noticed it, her forehead broke into a frown. How could Jyoti be such a fool? She could just shake her head with pity for Jyoti's stupidity. There would never be another telephone call like that. Jyoti's father had his own chartered accountant's firm. Jyoti was second in the hierarchy in a firm with a British name. Neepa's husband was an important officer in the Customs. Tuli's fiancé, Tony Kapadia, had his own agency exporting Indian silk batik, carpets, brass Natarajas, and Bankura terracotta horses. Jyoti's father-in-law lived in Britain.

There was no one in the family any more to do something out of the ordinary and provide an occasion for a sudden message on the telephone that would drag Sujata to Kantapukur to identify a dead body in the morgue.

There was no one in the family any more to be such a fool as to send Jyoti and Jyoti's father running through the corridors of power while Sujata and Tuli were the only ones who could be spared to rush to Kantapukur.

There was no one in the family any more to commit a crime that could leave him lying dead in Kantapukur. The dom,[1] removing the heavy sheet. The OC[2] asking, Do you identify your son?

They were all prudent people, they lived by the laws of the land, they were good citizens. They would never drag Sujata into a situation like that. They would never drive Jyoti's father to desperation. Jyoti's father had had to pull so many strings to hush up the news that his son had died such a scandalous death.

When the message came over the telephone, his first concern was how he could keep the news from the people who knew him. Going to Kantapukur to identify the body did not seem that important. He had brought up Jyoti, his eldest, according to his cherished ideals, and in the fitness of things he had accompanied his father on the same mission.

Dibyanath had not allowed Sujata to take his car. It would not be the right thing to keep his car waiting before Kantapukur. Anybody could identify the car.

That day, with Brati's death, Brati's father had also died for Sujata. The way he had behaved that day, that moment, had shattered numberless illusions for her. It had burst upon her with explosive force. Like one of those massive meteors crashing upon the ancient world billions of years ago. Like one of those explosions that broke up the solid mass of the earth into continents separated by the oceans.

Dibyanath never knew that his behaviour on that day had taken him far away from Sujata, that he was dead for

Sujata from that day onwards. He lay in a bed next to Sujata's but he never knew that he did not exist for Sujata from that day when he had placed his own position and his own security before the dead Brati.

Dibyanath had succeeded in his mission, his string-pulling. The next day the newspapers reported the deaths of four young men. Their names were reported. Brati was not mentioned in any of the reports.

That was how Dibyanath had wiped Brati away. But Sujata had never been able to do that.

Sujata knew very well that nothing like that would ever happen in the house again. And that was why she found it funny that Jyoti should have the telephone removed to his room.

Bini had noticed the mocking wisp of a smile on her face and had broken into tears. She told Jyoti, She has no heart.

What Bini had said was meant for Sujata's hearing. Sujata had heard the words but they had not hurt her. She had always felt, and she felt it again, Bini must have loved Brati.

That was the last time that she had felt that Bini loved Brati. She did not find Brati's photograph on the corridor wall. She did not see Brati's old shoes. Brati's raincoat, too, had disappeared.

Bini, where's the picture?

In the room on the second floor.

In the room on the second floor?

Father said . . .

Father said?

She was not shocked to find Dibyanath still trying to wipe Brati out, even after his death. It was no new grief for her. She felt that it was quite characteristic of Dibyanath to take a decision like that. But couldn't Bini protest and stop it?

Sujata had not said a word. She had left home for the bank quietly. She had been working at the bank for quite some time now. She had joined when Brati was three. Brati's father had been facing some problems at his office. They had lost two important accounts.

That was when Sujata took up her job. The family had encouraged and supported her. Even her mother-in-law had said, You should have begun earlier. It was Dibu's generosity that he did not send you to work earlier.

Nobody had cared to understand why Sujata wanted to work, why she had made all the enquiries herself and found a job for herself. Dibyanath and his mother constituted the centre of attraction in the home. Sujata had a shadowy existence. She was subservient, silent, faithful and without an existence of her own.

She knew people at the bank. Otherwise the job would not have come her way. It was her family connections, her aristocratic bearing and the way she pronounced her English that brought her the job. For there were lots of women looking for a job, with a BA from Loreto College!

But it was Brati alone who missed her and cried.

In her dreams, a three-year-old Brati still clasped her around her knees. He sobbed and nagged, Ma, don't go to office today, just this one day, why can't you stay with me?

Fair, thin, Brati, silky hair, eyes full of warmth. The same Brati whose name appeared after one thousand and eighty-three names in the list of the dead in what was known as the Decade for Liberation. But if you collected the names of the dead in the first two years and a half of the decade, would you come across Brati's name? If you relied on the newspapers for your source of information, you would never know about Brati.

Brati's father had seen to it that his name did not appear in the newspapers.

Brati Chatterjee?

How are you related?

No, you won't see his face.

Identification mark?

A mole on the throat?

You don't have to see the face.

What had she said that day? Did she say, I want to see his face? She had identified the blue shirt, the fingers, the hair. Did she still have any doubts? Had doubt defied all evidence, all reason, to insist on a sight of the face? Was that why Sujata had said . . . ?

The dom had felt pity for her, and asked, What will you see, Maiji? Is there anything left of his face?

What had Sujata done then? There were four other corpses lying there. Somebody went on crying somewhere. Somebody struck her head on the floor. She did not remember the faces any more. They were now all lost in a mist, but there were memories that glowed bright, hard, luminescent, like a diamond knife. There were three bullet holes on his body, one on the chest, one on the stomach, one on the throat. Blue holes. The bullets had been aimed from close range. The skin around the holes was blue. The cordite had left its burns. Chocolate-coloured blood. The cordite had scalded the skin around the hole to leave it parched and cracked into hollow rings.

Three bullet holes: on the neck, on the abdomen, on the chest.

Brati's face, Brati's face! She gathered all her strength together to pull the sheet away. Brati's face. Brati's face, battered and smashed by the blunt edge of a sharp, heavy weapon. She could hear Tuli stifling a shriek.

Sujata bent down to take a closer look at the face. She would have liked to caress his face with her fingers. She would have liked to call him by his name, Brati, Brati, and run her fingers over his face. But there was not an inch of skin left smooth and clear to bear the touch of her fingers. It was all raw flesh, all battered and smashed. Then she covered up the face. She turned around and blindly clasped Tuli to herself.

When she went back to the bank again, she remembered even as she left home that Brati's father had given instructions for Brati's picture to be removed.

Everyone stared at her at the bank. There was a sudden lull in the conversation the moment they saw her, then silence.

Luthra, the agent, was the first to come up to her.

Madam, so sorry . . .

Thank you. Sujata did not look up.

Memsaab.

A glass of water. Bhikhan held it out.

Memsaab!

Bhikhan spoke softly. One of Sujata's old habits. Every day, the first thing at office, she would have a glass of water.

In his eyes Sujata could read anguish and sympathy. Bhikhan seemed to be trying to enclose her within his looks. She had clasped Bhikhan to herself, the day there was a telegram carrying news that Bhikhan's son was dead.

Sujata had turned her eyes away from Bhikhan's. She could not bear his sympathy right then. Bhikhan, excuse me. Brati's death and the death of your son have been so unlike. Your son's death was of a kind that could make one forget that you were a bearer[3] and could draw one to hold you close to oneself.

But Brati died so differently. There were so many questions before his death, and so many after. Question marks. Rows and endless rows of question marks. Then, even while the questions remained unanswered, with not a single question answered, the file on Brati Chatterjee was closed for ever, so abruptly.

Please excuse me, Bhikhan.

The whole day she worked mechanically. In the evening, when Brati's father came home, she asked,

Have you asked them to remove Brati's portrait to the second floor?

Yes.

Brati's shoes?

Yes.

Why?

Why!

Dibyanath had just shaken his head. If Sujata refused to see why it was necessary to remove Brati's things, to wipe out Brati's existence and everything that bore his memory, was there anyone who could make her see reason?

Dibyanath had not said a word.

Is the room on the second floor locked?

Yes.

Who has the keys?

I have them.

Give me the keys.

Sujata had taken the keys and gone upstairs. Brati used to sleep in the room on the second floor. That had been the arrangement from when he was eight. At first he would refuse to sleep by himself. He was afraid to sleep alone. Sujata had suggested that Hem could sleep on the floor in the room.

But Dibyanath was angry. Sujata had not shown weakness with Jyoti, Neepa and Tuli, that was his argument. Sujata had said that she had had her objections when he had made arrangements for them also. For they, too, had been scared. But Sujata had not known then that one could in fact go against Dibyanath's wishes.

Brati was haunted by fears, the fears that haunt an imaginative child. A funeral procession in the night shouting 'Haribol!'[4] was frightening, the street performer masquerading as a bandit was frightening. But then he outgrew all his fears.

Brati was now beyond all fears and all daring.

From his childhood itself Brati loved to read poems about death. In Sujata's dreams Brati at seven sat on the windowsill, reading poetry, his legs dangling outside. When Sujata saw Brati in her dreams these days, a part of her mind would insist that it was just a dream. Brati did not exist. It was just a dream.

The other part of the mind went on insisting that it was not a dream, it was real.

In Sujata's dreams Brati still sat on the windowsill, reading poems, his legs dangling outside, and Sujata sat on Brati's bed, listening. And even as she listened, she tidied up Brati's sheets, his pillow.

Brati read—

The one who was most scared

Was the one who unlocked the room of darkness.

She could see in her dreams Brati moving around, reading from his copy of *Shishu*.[5]

You left on a dark night.

Why don't you come back in secret on a dark night again?

Nobody will see you.

For they look for you only in the stars.

In her sleep Sujata cried out for Brati and then she would come awake. The dreams seemed so real, so irresistibly real, that Sujata would wake with a start and start looking for Brati.

Sujata stood at the door of the room on the second floor. Brati's bed with the bedclothes removed. His clothes in the cupboard. The portrait on the wall. Books on the shelves. Only the suitcase was missing, for the police had taken it away.

As she stood holding on to the bedstead, Sujata screwed up her eyes as she tried to think out how, maybe even indirectly, she had been responsible for the killing of Brati. Was there anything in the way she had brought up Brati that had made him into number 1084 in the decade that headed towards liberation? Or was there something that she could have done, or not done, to make him number 1084? Where did she fail?

Dibyanath could not stand Brati. He said,

Mother's child! It's you who taught him to be my enemy.

It took Sujata by surprise. Why should she tell Brati to be an enemy to his father? Why should she? Was Dibyanath Sujata's enemy? Didn't Sujata share Dibyanath's attachment to respectability, comfort and security? She had never even asked herself whether she shared these ideals or not. Surely she would have, if she had ever had any doubts on these issues?

Sujata came from a rich family, from an orthodox family. She had been put into Loreto College, made to do her graduation, only as a preparation for marriage. The bridegroom chosen was not rich, but he came from a well-known family. Sujata's father knew that he would go far.

Sujata held unquestioningly to all those values, comfort, security and all that went with them. And therefore the allegations that Dibyanath brought against her were unfounded.

If his allegations were false, all that it proved was that Sujata could not have asked Brati to be an enemy to Dibyanath. But it was not enough to prove that Brati did not consider his father an enemy. Sujata knew that Brati could not stand his father. She knew that quite well.

But why, Brati?

The individual who goes by the name of Dibyanath Chatterjee is not my enemy.

Then?

All the things and values he holds on to. There are many others who swear by the same things and values. The class that nurtures these values, we consider it our enemy. He belongs to that class.

I can't understand you, Brati.

You needn't try to understand. Why don't you fix the button?

Brati, you are changing.

How?

You are changing.

How can I help changing?

Where do you roam about the whole day?

I sit and talk.

With whom?

With friends.

Here's your shirt. You needed to have your buttons fixed before you could make a little time to talk to your mother?!

Brati had not said a word. He had screwed up his eyes and smiled. There was something new in his smile, in the manner he spoke. Tolerance, patience. As if he knew even before Sujata spoke a word that she could not understand what he said. He would treat Sujata like a child, would sound almost fatherly. Brati seemed to be pampering her. Sujata could feel a distance yawning between them, and Brati fast becoming a stranger. She suffered a lot. But how could she remain unsuspecting? How could she remain untouched by fear?

Why did it never strike her that when a son became a stranger to his mother, and they lost touch with each other even while they lived under the same roof, there could be a threat growing from it?

Sujata stood in Brati's room, screwed up her eyes, and brooded.

If Brati had died of some incurable sickness like Sujata's elder brother, there could have been questions remaining to be answered after his death. Questions like: Was the doctor to blame, or the people of the house? Could a different doctor have made a difference? Could a different medicine have made a difference? These are the questions that are asked when somebody dies of sickness.

If Brati had died in an accident, then the questions would have been different. People would have asked if Brati could have been a little more careful and averted the accident, or if the circumstances could have been influenced in any way. If Sujata had had Dibyanath's faith in horoscopes, the questions would have been: Was there any warning against death by accident? If there had been the hint of a warning, was there no suggestion of a preventive?

If Brati had paid the price of having been involved in a criminal offence, then there would have been the question as to who led Brati to commit the offence. How could he have strayed from the path determined for a member of this particular family? What are the measures that could have been adopted to prevent such an outcome?

But Brati did not come under any of these categories. All that Brati could have been charged with was that he had lost faith in the social system itself. Brati had decided for himself that freedom could not come from the path society and the state followed. Brati had not remained content with writing slogans on the wall, he had come to commit himself to the slogans. There lay his offence. Dibyanath and Jyoti had not offered the dead Brati the lighted stick to set his body aflame on the funeral pyre. Brati and those like him were such antisocials that their corpses would lie at the Kantapukur morgue. In the dead of the night pile upon pile of corpses would be taken to the burning ghat under police protection. Then they would be burnt.

The corpses burn bit by bit in the night. Those who believe in the traditional rituals associated with the dead can't hold their ceremonials in the morning as the holy books require. They have to wait the whole day, their eyes red and dilated. In the night they have to plead with some hanger-on of a priest, one of those that stick around the cremation grounds, to conduct the rituals. The brahman would charge a fixed fee per head and get through the ceremony in a rush.

Brati had written posters with slogans. When the police had searched his room, Sujata had seen the texts of the slogans. They were all in Brati's handwriting.

The Prison's our University.

From the Barrel of the Gun . . .

This Decade will be the Decade of Liberation.

Hate the Moderate, mark him, destroy him.

. . . is turning into Yenan today.

She had heard that Brati and his friends wrote their slogans on paper first, before writing them on the walls. They wrote on the walls in the dark of the night. Those who were desperate like Kalu would brave the ominous might of the police who lay in a circle around the locality, even while the blood of the dead Tapan lay spattered on the street, at eleven in the morning, to splash the clean wall of a rich citizen's house with slogans in red paint: The Red Blood of our Red Comrade Red Tapan of Red Bengal . . . Burn the Police Headquarters to . . .

The sentence remains unfinished as Kalu is hit by a bullet. It stays like that.

Brati and his friends belong to a new generation. They write slogans on the wall knowing full well that the slogans draw bullets. They are in a mad rush to reach Kantapukur.

Sujata had not been able to find a category of criminals to put Brati into.

Even as they cried for the dead Brati, Jyoti and Dibyanath had tried to make her see that the killers in society, those who adulterated food, drugs and baby food, had every right to live. The leaders who led the people to face the guns of the police and found for themselves the safest shelters under police protection, had every right to live. But Brati was a worse criminal than them. Because he had lost faith in this society ruled by profit-mad businessmen and leaders blinded by self-interest. Once this loss of faith assailed a boy, an adolescent, or a youth, it did not matter whether he was twelve, sixteen or twenty-two, death was his portion.

Death was the sentence reserved for everyone of them, for all those who had rejected a society of spineless, opportunist time-servers masquerading as artists, writers and intellectuals.

They were all sentenced to death. Anybody was permitted to kill them. People in all the parties, people of all creeds had the unlimited, democratic right to kill these young men who had rejected the parties of the establishment. To kill them one did not need any special sanction from the law or the courts of justice.

Individuals and gangs of killers had equal right to kill these faithless young men. They could be killed with bullets, knives, hatchets, spears, with any weapon whatsoever. They could be killed any time any place for any spectator present. Jyoti and Dibyanath had explained all this to Sujata. But Sujata had gone on shaking her head in denial.

No.

The question that preceded Brati's death was why Brati had come to place such absolute faith in the cult of faithlessness.

The question that followed his death was whether by killing him the authorities had been able to destroy the burning faith in faithlessness that Brati and his compatriots had stood for. Brati was dead. His friends were dead. But did that mean the end of the cause?

The questions remained: Was Brati's death futile? Did his death stand for a massive NO?

Was everything a fantasy? His conviction, his courage, his irresistible passion? The way he fooled Sujata on that sixteenth of January, leaving home in his blue shirt to warn Somu, Bijit, Partha and Laltu, even when he knew that it meant death? The way he looked at Sujata before he left? The way he studied the lines of agony on Sujata's beautiful, dignified, ageing face to etch them in his mind?

Sujata had gone on shaking her head in denial. She had locked the door of the room and come out. The key had remained with her from that day itself. In her bag. For these two years it had grown into a habit with Sujata to get up in the night and go to the room. She would clean the room, dust the furniture. She had relaid the bedclothes and kept his shoes at the foot of the clothes-rack. Folded and settled his clothes. There must be thousands of mothers like her who fondled their sons' clothes in secret and touched their sons' portraits lovingly.

Sujata sat in Brati's room. She spoke to Brati. She imagined Brati standing close to her. She thought of all the mothers who had to call their sons in secret and feel their closeness in secret.

Sujata spoke to Brati. There were times when Brati answered, there were times when he did not.

The telephone rang in Jyoti's room. All these thoughts crowded on her mind as Sujata crossed over to lift it up.

There was no telephone in the houses where Somu, Laltu, Bijit and Partha lived. There would be no telephone ringing to awaken those who lived in those houses. What could the mothers of Somu, Bijit and Partha be thinking this morning?

Bini, in a nylon nightie, opened the door. Her face was resentful. She hated rising early. She never seemed to get over her sleep.

Jyoti and Bini needed regular sleep and rest. Sujata's eldest son and his wife were deeply in love. They had separate beds from the time Suman was eight months old. Still, they had a reputation as a loving couple. Sujata had always valued a flesh and blood happiness. But Bini and her husband had successfully separated a flesh-and-blood happiness from love.

They believed in a love which was different. They had to have an orgy of a party to celebrate their marriage anniversary. They were always together, visiting or just enjoying themselves of an evening. Sujata had heard that

Bini never danced with anyone but Jyoti at the club. Bini had a reputation in society. Sujata lifted the receiver.

Who's it?

It's Nandini.

Nandini?

Yes, I'm back.

When?

Day before yesterday.

I see.

I must see you. I won't go to your place. Will you be going to the bank today?

No, I won't be going today, Nandini. It's my youngest daughter Tuli's engagement today.

Then?

It's for you to say where we can meet. Any time except the evening will do.

Four o'clock then?

Fine. Where should I go?

I'll give you an address. It's not very far from your place.

Tell me.

Nandini gave the address. Sujata replaced the receiver. Nandini! Brati was in love with Nandini. But Sujata had never seen Nandini.

Sujata looked at Jyoti. Only when Jyoti slept did Sujata see a semblance of Brati's features in his face.

She came out on to the corridor. It was cold outside. Nandini and Brati had published a poetry journal together. They had acted in a play together, but Sujata had had a bout of chickenpox at the time, and had not been able to go. Nobody had gone from the house. It was Hem alone who had said, the little one was cheered by the whole audience. They all clapped. They were all praising him. Hem was the only one who chatted with Brati. When Brati was fast growing into a stranger for Sujata, when she looked at his face and did not dare speak to him, it was Hem who would say, I know you're going out on a most important assignment, but a little grub should not come in the way!

It was Hem who had packed his suitcase for him when he had said that he was going to Digha, and had dropped off the bus on the way and gone somewhere else.

It was Hem who had said, Ma, the little one has a girlfriend. The cook had seen the girl waiting for the little one and going off together with him. The girl's dark.

That was Nandini. Why was Sujata in such a flutter? Was it because she had not slept the whole span that one should after a dose of Baralgan? Or was it because Nandini had rung up?

Bini came out of the bathroom, all dressed up. A crop of unruly hair cut at shoulder height. A blue, nylon cardigan over a blue sari. Bini knew how to match colours. So did Neepa, and Tuli too. Bini looked calm and graceful.

Who was it, Ma?

Nandini.

Nandini?

A friend of Brati's.

Bini looked curious.

Why are you going downstairs, Ma?

I have to look to things. Wake up Suman. He has to go to school. The bus will be here soon.

Tuli is downstairs already.

Sujata smiled. There was an engagement party for Tuli in the evening. Still she had to supervise the breakfast, the lunch, the arrangements for the evening, everything about the house. Tuli would not trust anybody.

At sixteen Tuli gave up studies to take a course in crafts. She took over the responsibility of running the household at the same time. When his chartered accountant's firm came to stability, Dibyanath had asked Sujata to give up her job. But Sujata had insisted on carrying on. Her mother-in-law was alive till Brati turned eight. As long as she had been alive, Sujata had never had the right to buy a sari of her choice.

That was why it was so important for Sujata to have a life of her own, going to office and coming back on her own. She would not think of giving up her job.

Tuli had her grandmother's features and nature. Her father and grandmother had resented Sujata's decision to stick to her job. Mother and son would go on complaining that Sujata wanted to be independent, that she did not like to share the responsibilities of running the household or bringing up children.

Tuli said the same things even now. She said that when the mother insisted on staying out of the house ten hours a day, the daughter had to look after everything. If I don't do it, who will?

Tuli was resentful, disgruntled all the time. When she poured tea into a cup or gave instructions to the cook she bore the look of a martyr. One only hoped she would change once she got married.

After a course in crafts, she had set up a shop with a friend, to print saris. That was how she came to know Tony

Kapadia. It was Tony's mother who had decided to announce the engagement formally on Brati's birthday. Swamiji, Mrs Kapadia's guru, lived in the United States. He had chosen the date as an especially auspicious one. According to his calendar. The Swami's disciples followed the Swami's special calendar, a calendar that did not list any holidays. All the three hundred and sixty-five days were reserved for karma and dhyana.[6] Once Tony's mother had received the guru's advice, neither Dibyanath nor Tuli had cared to consult Sujata.

As Sujata came down, she felt that Tuli must have fought with her silently for a long time. It was a very special day in Tuli's life. And she was angry that Sujata did not appear to be giving it much importance. Anything to eat, Mother?

Just a little fresh lime and water.

Why? Do you have the pain again?

No. It doesn't pain any more.

I just don't see why you have to take chances. An operation for appendicitis is so common these days.

Not always. An operation of the appendix should be elective. It should be removed at the slightest pain, before it showed an inflammation or signs of festering. That didn't happen with Sujata. The doctor suspected Sujata's appendix to be gangrenous. If it was not removed at the proper time, it could develop gangrene. It could be worse if it burst. But Sujata did not have a strong heart, she suffered from anaemia, it would not be wise for her to have an operation. All this Sujata had learnt only the day before. But all that was not for Tuli. She only said,

I'll have it operated.

When?

After your wedding.

That will be in April.

Maybe I'll have it done before that. Hem! Hem!

What is it, Ma?

Give me a little fresh lime and water.

Sujata sat at the table.

Who was that ringing up so early?

Nandini.

Tuli flushed. Her forehead showed resentment. She rattled the spoon inside the teapot to check how thick the liquor had become. Then she spoke—Why can't we ring a bell for breakfast? Everyone should be at the table at the same time for tea. When everyone chooses to come down as and when, it's too damned inconvenient for me, for the rest of the household.

Sujata looked at Tuli with wonder. She had the exact tone that her mother-in-law used. Her mother-in-law could not stand her children relaxing, chatting while they dined. She would shout at them all the time. And they all submitted to her law. It was Brati alone, the child Brati, who had revolted. He would get up late. When he came down for breakfast, the plates would have been removed according to the rules of the table. Brati would go to the kitchen, sit on a low stool near Hem and eat there.

Strange house! Strange discipline!

Tuli barely concealed her disgust. She was only twenty-eight. Why did she have to be so resentful already? She still had her whole life lying before her.

Jyoti goes to sleep late. Why wake him up early? Your father doesn't take tea. He has his yoghurt . . .

I'm not talking about Baba. In fact, I've sent him his yoghurt already, the moment his masseur left.

Bini will be down once she has put the water and the flowers in the thakurghar.[7]

Silly sham!

Why should it be a sham? Your grandmother had her regular rites. I didn't like them. I only offered a few flowers, mechanically. But Bini believes in it, so she does puja. How can you call it a silly sham?

I'm sorry I don't understand. Born in Britain, lived there sixteen years, where she gets such piety from I don't know!

Her father had his own house in England, she grew up there. But where's the contradiction between growing up in Britain and offering flowers and water in the thakurghar? I don't see any.

It would've been different if she felt any true reverence. For her the thakurghar is mere interior decoration.

Don't you visit Swami's temple on Park Street?

That's different, Ma.

I don't see the difference. One believes in what one chooses to believe in. But how can you claim absolute rightness for whatever you believe in and write off what others believe in as mere sham?

Brati did the same. He mocked what others believed in.

Your faith in your Swami, and Bini's faith in her thakurghar come to the same thing. But the things in which Brati believed were quite different, Tuli. And anyway I don't remember Brati mocking. He challenged the beliefs of others, that's all you can say. When you couldn't cope with his arguments, you got wild. It was fun for him when you lost your temper.

How can you say he believed in things, Ma? He didn't believe in anything.

Tuli, I refuse to discuss Brati with you.

But why?

What's the use? You don't know Brati.

You will still go on . . .

Tuli! Keep quiet!

Sujata's hands were shaking. She put down the glass. A few unbearable moments. Then Sujata relaxed and said, Hem, ask Bini to come down for her tea.

Tuli, born of her womb, looked at her, her eyes the vicious eyes of a stranger, and almost hissed,

Do I have to go to the vault today to fetch the ornaments?

I'll go.

Will you be home in the evening?

Yes.

I hope you'll behave normally with Tony's friends today at least.

Have you . . . have you invited Saroj?

Yes, we've invited him. We don't know if he'll come.

Saroj!

Saroj Pal. Saroj Pal, No Pardon for You. Empty, empty threats. For two years Saroj Pal has conducted 'this massive investigation, search and punitive operation. His supreme efficiency and courage have been . . . '

Decade of Liberation, Decade of Liberation! It was left to Saroj Pal to organize the army against liberation. Like a real leader he sent out the orders: The cruel goddess, the dark goddess asks for blood! Saroj Pal, suave and sophisticated, handsome, the smile of a Prince Charming, a flawless intonation, Yes, Mr Chatterjee, I quite assure you . . . Mrs Chatterjee, I understand, I too have a mother. Saroj Pal. Yes, search the room. No, Mrs Chatterjee, your son lied to you, he didn't go to Digha. Broke his journey. Misguided youth! Yes, a cancerous growth on the body of democracy. No, Mr Chatterjee, there'll be nothing in the papers. You're Tony's future father-in-law, Tony is my . . . Saroj Pal.

Tuli went on staring at Sujata.

Enough is enough, Ma. You've turned this house into a tomb, Ma. Father doesn't dare say a word when you're about. Brother has a guilty look all the time . . . Everybody tries to hush up an incident like the one we had. That's natural. Brati is dead. You must think of the living. You . . .

Do they all try to hush things up that soon? Even before the dead body is identified? Does it have to happen like that? A father gets the message on the telephone and doesn't feel for a moment the urge to rush to see his dead son! The first thing that strikes him is that it would be unwise to keep the car waiting before Kantapukur?

Or maybe Brati was long dead to his father and his brother, long before the fatal message came over the telephone? Maybe that is why Sujata had found it hard to accept, and they had accepted it the very moment it burst upon them? And maybe that is why the two of them had rushed out immediately to pull strings to keep the news out of the newspapers?

Sujata could see the weird design of an absurd play unfolding relentlessly. They were all characters in the play.

Brati belonged to the family. But his cruel murder was an embarrassment for his father, brother and sisters, who did not know how they could explain his death to their social circle. Brati had not stopped to consider what difficulties he would create for his closest relations and he had brought a blight on the beautifully organized household. The man who had messed up their charming social game was now dead. And they counted Sujata as one of the dead man's party. They were the other party.

It's hard for a father, brother or sister to say this . . .

My son was . . .

See, my brother was . . .

My younger brother was a . . .

Tony, Brati . . .

Sujata belonged to the other camp, the camp of the enemy. For Sujata was the only one in the family who had never blamed Brati for messing up her neatly organized life. She had never blamed Brati. She had not beat her breast in wild wailing. She had never put her head on the chest of anyone of them and sought consolation. She had made up her mind quite early that she would never seek consolation from those who thought first of themselves while Brati lay dead in the morgue. She had felt closer to Hem than to Brati's father, brother or sisters.

Sujata could sense how they had put Brati into the other camp from the time Brati had begun changing. Brati would not act the way they acted. Brati would not follow in their footsteps even when he grew older, that they knew. And so Brati belonged to the other camp.

If Brati drank like Jyoti, if he could go about drunk like Neepa's husband, if he could flirt with the slip of a typist the way Brati's father did, if he could be a master swindler like Tony Kapadia, if he could be as loose as his sister Neepa, who lived with a cousin of her husband's, then they could have accepted Brati as one of them.

If they could count on Brati to join their game once he grew up, they would not have branded him as part of the other camp.

But Brati had never showed a sign of moving towards that direction. Sujata herself had never been unhappy in particular, with her children, her son-in-law, her husband—all behaving the same way. She had been taught by life to take things as they came. She had never thought of asking questions. She never knew that she had the right to ask questions. She had been hurt at times. Hurt badly. Dibyanath had always fooled around with women. His mother looked upon his indiscretions with indulgence. For her it was a mark of her son's virility; her son was no henpecked husband. Sujata was hurt. But she had consoled herself with the thought that nobody in life had uninterrupted happiness.

But Brati was different. Even as a child he would not be scared by false bogeys. He would listen to reason. He would never be intimidated by threats. As he grew up, Sujata could see a mind of a different cast opening up, a mind different from all those she had known, those she had identified with her husband and her other children.

Sujata tried to immerse herself in his life, as she read books with him, went to the zoo with him or spent long hours with his friends. Brati became for her the only legitimate excuse for going on living. Maybe, maybe, Sujata had become too possessive about Brati.

For Brati alone Sujata had defied her husband and her mother-in-law. She had not exposed Brati to the absurd disciplining and arbitrary indulgence that the other children had endured. Her mother-in-law had had her other children entirely under her command. But Sujata had held on to Brati. Sujata had given Brati all her care and all her love. He was stubborn, sensitive and imaginative. Sujata had had to strain a lot to protect Brati from the dominance of her husband and her mother-in-law.

Was that why they were still so implacable? Or do they bear a feeling of guilt towards Brati deep within themselves? And do they try to hide it with the roughness that Tuli shows or the guilty reserve that Dibyanath shows or the humility that is Jyoti's?

Sujata did not say any of this. She only said, Tuli, you will be very happy in life.

Afternoon

The colony that housed two hundred thousand people had not grown according to any plan. This was the first of the colonies in West Bengal where the residents had grabbed the land and settled down. In the beginning the landlord had a plot of land, a few garden plots, several pools and tanks, a few small villages.

After 1947, as more and more people moved in, the map of the region changed radically. The colony spread and spread till it had swallowed up the fields, the marshes, the coconut palm orchard, the cornfields, the villages.

The Opposition had always polled a majority of votes in the region. And the Government had taken its revenge by denying the region the simple comforts of a decent road, a health centre, an adequate number of tubewells or a bus route. Those who had grown rich in the last two decades in the region itself had not cared to do anything for the area.

The CMDA[8] has dug up the roads only recently in a spurt of developmental concern.

There is no longer any unrest or panic. No shops and markets suddenly pulling down shutters, no doors to houses being slammed shut, no rickshaw pullers, stray dogs and pedestrians running in a mad frenzy. Now you no longer hear exploding bombs, murderous shouts, the groans of the dying or the cheers of jubilant killers.

No black cars, helmeted policemen and gun-toting soldiers pursue some desperate lone young boy. Nor does one see bodies tied by rope to the wheels of police vans, still alive, being dragged and slammed against the asphalt.

One does not see blood on the streets, nor hear a mother's despairing lament these days. The lettering on the walls has been replaced by new slogans. Live Long, Comrade Mazumdar! Revolutionary Comrade! We'll never forget you! The killers who killed our youth will never be forgiven! The victors proclaimed their triumph through new slogans that covered the old ones completely.

Adolescents no longer shout slogans even as they die. There is no sign anywhere of the two-and-a-half years' disorder that had disrupted the even tenor of daily life here.

Happy and peaceful households are back. Rice is hoarded freely again and sold freely in the blackmarket. The cinemas draw crowds day and night. People throng temples where godmen reign, seeking salvation.

The killers of yesteryear have changed their garb and move about fearlessly in their new identities. A chapter has ended. A new chapter of the great saga has begun.

Only where narrow lanes meet do memorial tablets stand as tireless avengers, like ugly scars on a clean body. But these tablets do not carry the names of Somu, Bijit, Partha or Laltu. There is no question of their carrying

Brati's name. His name, their names, remain only in the hearts of a few. Perhaps.

Sujata sat in the house where Somu had once lived. She had already brought the ornaments from the bank vault. They were in her bag. At one time the ornaments had been allotted to Neepa, Bini, Tuli and Brati's future bride.

She had already given Neepa and Bini their portions.

Tuli had put in a claim for the portion put aside for Brati's future bride.

She would probably leave a few for Neepa's daughter and Jyoti's son, and give the rest away to Tuli.

Sujata herself never wore anything more than a slim bangle on her wrist, a pair of small earrings and a thin chain around her neck. She has never put on a coloured sari since Brati was born.

She looked tired, broken. Somu's mother sat before her, crying silently. Her frail, dark face was awash with tears. She had become thinner in the last one year. She wore a dirty coarse plain white sari.

It was a ramshackle house, with moss on the roof, cracked walls patched up with cardboard. Still, this was the only place where Sujata found some peace for herself. She felt as if she had come home.

The first time they had met, Somu's sister had broken into tears. But this time she only frowned. She had lost her father soon after Somu's death. Since then she had had to give tuition from morning till night in order to run the household. The fire of the cremation pyre burns up all the fat in the body. The fire of domestic responsibility had burned up Somu's sister. She bore a severe anger in her looks. Somu's dying had left her dead. He had been the only son in the family. Because he had to go to a good college, their father had not provided money for his sister's education. She paid for her own education by tutoring children.

Somu's sister gave her a hostile look and went out without saying a word. Sujata could see that she had taken over the job of running the household. She hated the idea of an outsider coming in once a year to remind them of her dead brother. Sujata felt utterly helpless. She looked at her pleadingly. She wanted to ask her not to shut the door that allowed her to come and go once in a while. But she could not say the words. Somu's sister went out.

Somu's mother was weeping. Sujata waited in silence.

They tell me, don't cry, Ma. He'll never come back. They tell me, why don't you think of the others? Think of Partha's mother. She lost Partha. And since then Partha's brother can't come home. He has to stay with his aunt or who knows where.

He isn't back yet?

No, Didi.[9] Those who died are lost anyway. But those who remain alive won't ever be able to come back home again. What kind of judgement is this, Didi?

Somu's mother went on weeping.

The first time she had come here, a year after it had happened, Sujata had had her hesitations. Somu's mother had been widowed only a few months ago. When she had come into the locality and asked for Somu's house the young men had looked at her with obvious surprise. At first they would not tell her. Finally someone pointed the house out—There.

Somu's mother kept staring, baffled, at Sujata's expensive white sari, aristocratic appearance and sophisticated ageing face encircled with greying hair.

I'm Brati's mother.

As the words hit her, the woman had cried out—My Somu!—and had raised a loud wail. Clasping Sujata to herself she said, It was your son, Didi, who came to warn them. He died for them. He knew Somu was back in his locality. He came and asked for Somu. He told me he had a message for Somu, and he would leave immediately. I stopped him, It's night; it's not safe to go through the colony. I asked him to stay the night and leave early in the morning. But there was no morning for them. That night, Didi, in this little room of ours, Somu and Partha and Brati slept close to one another.

This room?

This room.

There's no other room, really. My daughter went out with her sisters to sleep on the ledge outside. There's a fence to the ledge. The boys stayed inside. I sat at the window to keep watch.

Brati was here?

Yes, Didi. My dead husband was a poor shopkeeper, he didn't have any capital. He had a stall selling exercise books, pencils and slates. It had taken him a lot to raise this house. So the boys kept to the corner. Somu's father wouldn't sleep, he stayed awake to wake them up early in the morning. They talked and talked and laughed and laughed as they lay on my torn mattress. Didi, Brati's laughing face floats before my eyes. Your son had a complexion of gold!

Brati used to come here often?

Very often. He used to come, and ask for water, for tea, and what a sweet way he had about him.

Brati used to come here. He had tea here, he chatted, he spent so much of his time here.

Sujata looked at Somu's mother, their room, the picture on the wall torn from a calendar, the cup with its handle broken, with new eyes.

Brati, blood of her blood, the child whose birth had endangered her life, the young man who had become so strange and impregnable to her, was coming back to Sujata again.

She could still see Brati in her dreams, putting on a blue shirt, combing his hair. Or looking at her.

Studying her face.

When, after a long, sleepless night, her eyes would shut in sheer exhaustion, Brati stood at the bottom of the stairs looking up into her eyes. Sujata pleaded, Brati, don't go away. Brati kept looking at her. Sujata called out to him, Brati, why don't you come up? Brati kept looking. He did not speak, his lips did not smile.

But here Brati would speak, laugh, ask Somu's mother to make some tea, to give him a glass of water.

Somu's mother was saying, I used to tell him, why do you waste your life like this, my child? You have everything. A well-known father, a mother so learned. He wouldn't say a word. He would only smile. His smile floats before my eyes, Didi.

It hurt Sujata. Brati's smile, that wonderful smile. She had thought that all the memories were hers alone. Why had she never known that Brati had left memories to Somu's mother too?

Brati had been home that day. He sat in his room on the second floor writing who knows what. It was only later that Sujata discovered that he had been drafting slogans to be written on the walls. They took the papers away when they came to search his room. The papers were no longer in the house.

All that now remained in the house were books and exercise books, books received as prizes, gold medals, a snapshot with friends in Darjeeling, a pair of running shoes, a cup from a sports meet. All from Brati's days in school and college. Mementoes of a few years in Brati's life. They brought back memories to Sujata. Ma, I'll get a prize. Won't you be there? The day Brati went to the park nearby to become a member of the Boys' Club.[10] The Independence Day parades when he marched so proudly with the boys, beating on the drums, playing on the bugles. The day he had come back with a cup from the football finals, and a fractured leg.

There was nothing from the days when he had begun to change—they had cleared away, without a trace, the books, papers, leaflets, sheets with revolutionary slogans, journals from that last one year. Sujata had been told that all these were burnt as a rule.

Brati was home all day. Sujata was quite surprised to see him when she came home from the bank. It was only later that she knew that he had been waiting all day for a call. He knew that Somu and his group would go back to their locality. A message had been sent, asking them not to go back. But Brati did not know then that the person who carried the message would not take it to Somu and his friends, but would carry it straight to those who waited to trap and kill them. When the call came in he knew there was a crisis.

That was how they died. By trusting too many people. Brati and his fellow workers never realized that those they trusted could be tempted with offers, jobs for some, security for others, a happy life for still others. They never realized that there were many who had joined them only with the aim of betraying them. Brati was young. The passion of a belief had blinded them to the reality. They had not realized that the system against which they fought had the capacity to contaminate even the child in the womb. Brati and his compatriots had believed unquestioningly that all the young men were devoted to the cause, that they could all defy death. And so Brati had believed that the message must have reached Somu and his group. He waited for the call only to assure himself that the group was safe.

When the whole day passed and evening came— winter evenings come early in Calcutta—Brati must have realized that if the news was to have come at all it should have reached him by now. When there was no call by afternoon, he began to have doubts. Afternoon turned to evening, then it became dark. Sujata came back.

You didn't go out today?

No.

Why?

Just like that. Come, let's have tea.

They had tea together. Brati sat with his back to the door. He had an old shawl wrapped around himself. It was bluish in colour, covered with small holes. When Brati stayed home in winter, he wrapped it round himself. Sujata would often say, Take that off, Bapu. Put on something else.

Brati would say, It's very 'awm', as Hem would say.

That was the shawl Brati had on, his hair uncombed, the door behind him gaping wide, beyond it the wall at the end of the courtyard, the tap where the utensils were washed.

Over tea, after a long time, Brati was teasing Bini. Brati had been to Digha a few days ago with his friends. Sujata learnt later that he had never gone to Digha. She learnt that the police had converged on the station at Kharagpur. The military police, wearing helmets, were getting into the buses on the route to Digha, and examining the faces of the passengers in the glare of their torches. The bus was forced to move in slow motion through certain villages. There were policemen on guard on both sides of the road to Digha, with their bayonets gleaming in the darkness. Brati didn't go to Digha.

Sujata did not know this then. Neither did Bini. She was asking him about Digha.

Brati said, Digha is a nasty place. No proper place to stay, no decent joint for a meal.

But my cousin's been there. She never complained.

She's your cousin, isn't she?

As if you don't know her! She plays tennis with your great pal, Dipak. Don't you hang around Dipak's place?

How would I know your cousin?

Sujata said, You needn't know her. But since you've been to their place, you must have noticed her.

Why?

Because she is a beauty.

More of a beauty than you?

Bini butted in—Ma, he's flattering you. He must have something up his sleeve.

Oh no, Bini. He doesn't need his cinema allowance any longer, nor his pocket money. He doesn't need to flatter his mother any more. In fact he doesn't even need his mother any more!

What a thing to say, Ma!

You're a fool, Ma, said Bini. I'd have grabbed his National Scholarship money the moment it came.

It's not that easy, Boudi,[11] you can ask Dada[12] and find out for yourself.

Why should I ask your brother?

Dada was a fool. He would spend his pocket money and borrow from the little stock I had saved from the money I got when I had my sacred thread ceremony.[13] I collected my interest when he returned the loan.

Sujata could sense Brati evading the question. She had asked him, Do you need your mother at all? Do you ever try to know what your mother feels and thinks? You're always running away, always slipping away. You have assignments all the time, you say.

I do have assignments.

Baba re baba! So many? Already? How will you manage when you have a serious job like your brother?

Brati had retorted, Why do you think my job is not serious?

Is gossiping a serious job?

Isn't gossiping serious business?

Yes, Sir, yes. And I know something else.

What do you know?

I know it's absolutely serious when you gossip with Nandini.

Who told you I gossip with Nandini?

Why should anybody have to come and tell me? Don't I answer the phone when Nandini calls?

Brati had broken into a smile. His silent smile. The eyes smiling. His face was dazzling. He smiled to parry an uncomfortable question.

Let's have a game of Ludo, Ma.

Bini said once again, Ma, Brati must definitely have something up his sleeve today.

Why don't you join us?

Oh no, I can't. I have to go out with Tuli. She'll get wild if I ditch her.

Why go when you don't want to?

Brati had sounded soft but firm.

Sujata and Brati had gone upstairs and played a game of Ludo. Sujata had asked him, Brati, who is Nandini?

A young woman.

Won't you let me see her?

If you want to.

I want to see her.

You won't like her.

Why?

She's no beauty.

So what?

Boss won't like her.

Behind his back, Brati called his father Boss. From the time he had become aware, he must have heard the set phrase—I am the boss in this house; what I say goes—thousands of times.

So what?

Ma, do you know where Boss goes every day after five?

Sujata guessed that Brati may know about the affair Dibyanath was having with the typist.

Why ask me that all of a sudden, Brati?

Just like that. Do you know?

Let it be, Brati.

Brati concentrated on the game for some time. Then he said, Ma, do I make you suffer?

Why should I suffer, Brati?

Just tell me, Ma.

I don't suffer, Brati.

Every now and then I get the feeling you suffer because of me. You don't suffer over Dada or my sisters.

Sujata had not replied. Sujata could never lie or hide things.

Why don't you answer?

What do you mean by suffering, Brati?

If you suffer, that's suffering.

How can I expect everyone to be the way I would like them to be? They are like themselves. If they are happy, I am content.

Are they happy?

That's what they say.

Strange!

What's strange?

Why are you so passive, Ma?

What else can I do? I was trained to be passive about my children. Your father, grandmother . . .

Dibyanath had not allowed Sujata the most common rights that a mother has. His mother held the reins. Dibyanath never knew that one could honour one's mother without humiliating one's wife. His wife under his feet, his mother held aloft. That was his ethos.

With her pride and strong sense of dignity, Sujata had realized soon after her marriage, that the more she kept herself aloof from the household, the more satisfied the others were. Dibyanath and her mother-in-law were the 'others'. Jyoti, Tuli and Neepa had always known their mother in a subsidiary role. They had never had to take account of her. In Sujata's mind, one day they had joined the ranks of the others.

Of course, Dibyanath never cared to probe into these deep wounds. He was neither very attached nor indifferent to his wife. The way he saw it, a wife had to love, respect and obey her husband. A husband was not required to do anything to win his wife's respect, love and loyalty. He had built a house of his own, he kept servants, and that was enough he thought. He never tried to make a secret of his affairs with young girls outside the house. He felt it was within his rights.

He was not inconsiderate, however. He had asked Sujata to give up her job the moment he found his firm paying well.

Sujata had stuck to her job. That was the second occasion on which she rebelled.

Dibyanath knew that his children were aware of his infidelities. It caused him no embarrassment. For he knew that his first three children would never defy him and that they considered all his actions part of his virility.

He had told Jyoti, Your mother is a bit puzzling. Why won't she give up her job? She is not one of those women itching for independence. She is not one of those who find it fashionable just to be working. So why won't she give up her job? Strange!

Have you asked Ma?

I told her, You needn't work any longer. Why don't you give up the job and look after the household? Mother is dead. She told me, When the children were younger and I'd have enjoyed looking after the household, I had nothing to do. I was not permitted to take up any responsibilities. Now your children have grown up. The household runs fine on its own. I don't think it needs anything from me.

Dibyanath had never understood Sujata. She was not one of those radicals, the independent woman conscious of her rights. She was not one of those fashionable ladies with fashionable jobs driving their own cars through Calcutta.

Sujata was quiet, taciturn and old-fashioned in appearance. She would rarely use the family car. She used the tram to go to the bank, and returned the same way. She went out rarely. She did not socialize with friends or relations. Back from office, she would do a little reading, water the plants and maybe chat for a while with her youngest son, if he happened to be there.

Refusing to leave her job was Sujata's second act of rebellion. Her first act of rebellion was when Brati was two. She had refused to be a mother for a fifth time.

Dibyanath had exploded. He had said, Once they marry, a husband and a wife have duties to each other. I don't see any reason why you should object.

No.

Sujata had refused firmly.

You are denying me my right.

You have never depended on me alone for your fulfilment.

What do you mean?

You and I both know what I mean.

All the time that Sujata had gone on submitting to Dibyanath, bearing his children, Dibyanath had gone on sleeping with other women. After Sujata's refusal, his sex life outside the house became more active. If that was a snare to make Sujata feel guilty, she did not fall for it.

The day before Brati's death she could have told all this to Brati. But she had not. Now she knew that Brati knew everything and understood everything. He watched his mother all the time. When he was only ten, he would rush back home from his games, whenever Sujata was sick. He would offer, Shall I sit here and fan you?

Dibyanath called him a milksop. Mother's boy. No manliness. But in the manner of his dying, Brati proved his indomitable strength and courage.

That day Brati had sat looking at her for a long time. Then he had said, Let's stop the game. Why don't we chat for a while?

Just a minute. Let me run down to the kitchen and tell them what to cook.

Isn't Chhot-di[14] around?

No, Tuli's busy with Tony's exhibition. She'll just drop in to collect Bini.

Right.

What do you want for dinner tomorrow?

Why, suddenly?

Isn't it your birthday tomorrow?

Really! How do you remember birthdays?

How can I help it?

I never remember.

But I never make a mistake.

So you'll make special payesh for me.

That's all I do these days for birthdays, anyway.

Wait. Let's think. What can you make for me?

Don't ask for meat.

Why? Is Boss dining at home?

Yes.

Make whatever you like.

The phone rang as Sujata went downstairs. She saw Brati lifting the receiver as she left.

She came up. Looked. Brati had on a blue shirt and trousers, and was combing his hair.

What's the matter?

I have to go out. Could you give me some money?

Where are you going?

Some business. Could I have the money?

Here's the money. When will you be back?

I'll be back . . . back soon . . . Just a minute.

Brati dipped into the pockets of his trousers and rummaged about. A piece of paper he tore up into pieces.

Which way are you going?

There was no special fear at the back of her mind when Sujata asked the natural question. For Calcutta was in a different state those days. For the older people, for people over forty, any place in Calcutta was safe. But for the younger people, Calcutta had too many banned localities.

Only recently Sujata had been going through a pile of old newspapers, and had discovered with a shock all that had been happening in Calcutta two and a half years ago.

Back in those days, she had only felt something, everything, turning topsy turvy. When Brati was still alive and Sujata was yet to know that Brati belonged to the ranks of the doomed, she would read the papers and feel the shock of every bloody episode reported.

Nobody else in the house even looked at the papers at that time. They would say, All you see is gruesome descriptions of how many were killed, and how they were killed.

Since they were so repelled by the news, Sujata and Brati were the only ones who read the papers.

Sujata read the papers before she left for the bank. The city of Calcutta seemed wrong to her. It still had all its old landmarks—the Maidan, the Victoria Memorial, the Metro cinema, the Gandhi statue, the Monument. Still, it was not Calcutta. She did not recognize, did not know, this Calcutta.

She had gone back to the old newspapers later, and discovered that the morning the telephone rang in her room, the gold rates had gone up as usual, the banks in Calcutta had had transactions worth crores of rupees, an elephant cub was flown from Dum Dum to Tokyo carrying the Indian Prime Minister's best wishes for the children of Japan, a festival of European films opened in Calcutta, the radical artists and intellectuals of Calcutta demonstrated against barbarities in Vietnam, on Red Road and before the American Center on S. N. Banerjee Road.

Everything went on as usual, all that spelt normalcy in Calcutta's own terms, all that characterized Calcutta as India's most conscious city.

All this showed that things were quite normal in the city that day. Only, it was dangerous for Brati to go from Bhowanipur to South Jadavpur; in Barasat eight young men were first strangled and then shot dead before they could leave their locality. In east Calcutta, a group of young men seated the bloodstained corpse of a young boy who had grown up with them in a rickshaw, and escorted it with drums and a brass band, dancing alongside, like some divine idol being taken for immersion.

The radical citizens of Calcutta found nothing unnatural in the spectacle.

Exactly a year and three months later, the writers, artists and intellectuals of Calcutta turned West Bengal upside down out of sympathy with and support for the cause of Bangladesh. Surely they must have been thinking the right thoughts, and mothers like Sujata must have been on the wrong track altogether! If their radical consciences remained unaffected by a situation that did not allow the youth of West Bengal to move from one neighbourhood to another in the same city, they must have been right.

The deadly risks that the youth of West Bengal faced could not have been important enough. If they had been important, wouldn't the artists, writers and intellectuals of this legendary city of processions have picked up their pens?

Somu had twenty-three wounds on his body. Bijit sixteen. Laltu's entrails had been pulled out and wrapped around his body. All this surely could not have smacked of barbarity, of bestiality. If it had, then the poets and writers of Calcutta would have spoken of the barbarities on this side of the border along with those on that side of the border. Since they didn't, since they could ignore the daily orgy of blood that stained Calcutta and concentrate on the brutal ceremony of death beyond the border, their vision must have been flawless. Sujata's vision was surely wrong. Surely. The poets, writers, intellectuals and artists were honoured members of society, recognized spokesmen for the country at large.

Who is Sujata? Only a mother. Who are those hundreds of thousands whose hearts, even now, are being gnawed by questions? Only mothers.

When Brati in his blue shirt patted his hair smooth in his usual manner before leaving the house for ever, Sujata had asked him, Where are you off to?

Brati had paused for a second. Then he had smiled and said, Alipur. If I am late, you'll know I'm staying the night at Ronu's place. Don't worry.

Brati already knew that something terrible had happened. The messenger who was supposed to inform Somu and his group had not carried the information to them. Without the message, Somu and his group had gone back to their locality as decided in the original plan.

Brati did not know, however, that their messenger, instead of warning Somu and his group, had alerted those who waited in the locality for them, that they were on their way.

Brati thought he would meet Somu and his group that night itself and bring them safely out of the locality. He did not have much hope of success, and yet he had thought he might just manage.

Yet his 'Don't worry' had sounded so disarmingly normal and casual that Sujata had not been worried at all.

It was safe to be with Ronu.

Millie Mitter and Jishu Mitter's son Ronu's house was quite safe. Ronu was with Brati at school. In his own community, he was something of a rebel. Even as a student he had formed his own pop group to sing at cabarets. In his rebellion against society, he would smoke marijuana with the sahibs,[15] but he was safe.

Brati would be safe if he spent the night with Ronu. Sujata had told him, Tell Hem to shut the door. Don't forget to tell her.

I'll tell her.

Walking down the stairs, Brati had suddenly paused halfway. Sujata had sensed him stopping, and looked up. She came out on the verandah and looked at him. She found Brati staring at her. He was looking gravely, intently, into her face.

A mother's sixth sense, a mother's sixth sense—all nonsense! Sujata did not have the shadow of a premonition. If, as they say, a mother always knows beforehand, shouldn't she have sensed something was wrong?

No, she guessed nothing.

She came to know later that Ronu and Brati had been out of touch for about a year and a half. They no longer even had a mutual friend. Brati had lied to her.

While sleeping, Sujata's body slumbered, but her sensibility was sharper. In her sleep, Sujata often stood at the top of the staircase, Brati a few steps below her. In her dream, Sujata knew Brati would not go to Ronu's house, he would go to warn Somu and his group. In her dream,

Sujata yearned to rush out and drag Brati back by the hand. She yearned to scream out—Brati, come back!

She couldn't say a word. In her dream her feet turned to stone. Brati stared at her face, he waited, then when three holes glowed sharp and clear on Brati's throat, his stomach and his chest, tearing straight through his blue shirt, when the razor-edge scar railed from the back of the head down to the end of the neck, and the contours of his face changed before her eyes, Sujata was dragged back to reality. She woke up every time with the strange illusion that Brati had been with her all the time and had only just gone out.

The day Brati left she had had no fears, no premonitions. That night as usual she had given Dibyanath his nightly dose of digestive medicine. When Suman broke into a fit of crying, she brought him out and quietened him as usual. She reminded Hem that it was Brati's birthday the next day; she must remember to buy a litre of milk. To make payesh.

All the normal, daily chores.

Did Sujata know that that very night, before midnight, a crowd had gathered outside Somu's house? The elders of the locality, respectable, old gentlemen had raised the cry— Throw them out!

The first time Sujata stood before Somu's mother, sat in their room, it seemed to her that this was a normal household with normal human reactions.

She realized that Somu's mother, with her little learning, her limited intelligence and her inability to put her ideas into words, thought the same thoughts as she with all her learning, clarity of vision and competence in articulating ideas.

The thoughts that troubled her were cried aloud by Somu's mother—Why did they have to kill them, Didi? They could have maimed them but let them live! At least I would have known my Somu was alive! . . . He could have lived far from my sight. They could have kept him in prison. Still, at least I'd have known that he lived! Tell me why I've been punished like this!

Somu's sister had pleaded, Don't cry, Ma. He won't come back. He kicked you in the chest, Ma, and went off. Ma, look at me and pull yourself together.

I tell my heart, there's no use crying. But my heart won't understand.

What will you gain by crying your life away?

You are right. Didi, I am a doomed woman, doomed from birth. Even the wild foxes and dogs weep over my fate. My father married me off years ago. My man never had a chance to learn how to read or write. He was the eldest in the family. He had to run the household. Back in the old country he had a plot of fertile land. Here he had nothing. He was not the kind of man to grab whatever came his way and improve his lot. It was nothing but misery, misery, all the way.

Sujata could follow every word that Somu's mother spoke.

He had all his children educated. You can't do without education nowadays, Didi. He didn't have to spend anything on Somu's education. Somu won scholarships every year. It was due to his scholarships that he joined that college. Who are the people who showed him that path, who taught him to die? I would tell him over and over again— What are you up to? Where do you go off to? My son would say, Why are you so worried, Ma? What I'm doing is not evil. I didn't understand then.

Somu's didi asked, Mashima, would you like some tea?

A little, maybe.

Somu's mother said, This daughter of mine has given up college. She spends all her time giving tuition and learning typing. The younger one her aunt took away. Still there are two more. It's not easy, Didi, to feed four on what she earns from tuitions.

Somu's didi brought a cup of tea. Sujata had never had tea in such a cup.

It's all fate. My son grew up to become an adult. He would complete his studies and find a job and feed his parents, marry off his elder sister—that was how we had charted it out. But now will my daughter ever be able to wear sindoor[16] on her forehead?

Why do you think that way? Things will slowly get better. She's sure to get married some day.

Sujata had spoken the words with all sincerity. But Somu's mother could have taken them otherwise and flared up. One couldn't have blamed her if she had flared up. It was a cruel joke to put it like that, to say that Somu's sister would get married some day just like that—without a guardian, without money, without a soul to come to their assistance.

Somu's mother had not flared up. She had held Sujata's hands in her hands, and said, Bless her, Didi.

Then she went on again. Why did they have to come here? The four of them were living far from the locality. Why did they come back to die? Why did your son have to come to warn them and die with them? You have another son. You can hold him close and forget your loss. But he was my only son. As a child he almost died of typhoid. How I fought to keep him alive! Was it all for this?

Brati too had jaundice when he was in class ten. Brati had become gaunt and sallow. Food for Brati had to be carefully measured and cooked without a touch of spice. Sujata gave up all the delicacies that Brati was not allowed to have. The only meat he was allowed was chicken. That was the time Sujata gave up meat altogether. She had never gone back to it again.

Did the other boys belong to the neighbourhood?

They were all either from this locality or the neighbouring one. Bijit's elder brother has now taken his mother away to Kanpur. Partha's mother has broken down totally. The sickly woman collapsed under the shock and took to her bed. She lost one son to the God of Death, the other's in exile. If he ever comes back to the locality, he'll be cut into pieces, they say.

He's Partha's only brother?

Yes, Didi. Partha's mother doesn't leave her bed, refuses to eat and goes on crying—Give me back my sons! Is she going mad, Didi? A woman's life is like a tortoise's. She'll find peace only if she dies.

Wasn't there another one?

Laltu, you mean. He didn't have a mother to torment. She was dead already. Laltu was without a mother from the time he was born. When his father married again in his old age, Laltu was so angry that he shifted to his sister's. There was no one like him in the neighbourhood, he was brilliant in his studies, strong, the first to come forward whenever there was something useful to be done for the colony at large.

Did he live close by?

Two colonies away. Laltu, Partha, Bijit, Somu, they were all one of a kind. As long as they were around, no one in the locality could say or do anything evil. It was Laltu who inspired and instigated them all into the movement, and the unfortunate boy paid the price himself.

Sujata remembered having seen a number of dead bodies in the morgue. She had seen men and women lamenting over their dead at the cremation ground.

At the time she had not understood how those corpses, those grief-stricken men and women, were connected, were one with her. Now she realized that Brati had belonged with them not only in death, but also in life.

In that part of Brati's life which he had made by himself, where he was most himself, these boys were closest to him. Not the family. My son, my brother—these were just a set of dead definitions that Brati had carried with him through his life.

But Brati had built another Brati with his beliefs, his ideals and his ideology. This other Brati loved his mother, his mother loved him, but never really knew him. These boys knew the other Brati, the Brati that Sujata did not know. That was how they could be inseparable in both life and death. Just as Sujata found herself bound inseparably to all those who carried in their hearts the burden of their loss.

For a year after Brati's death, till she came down to see Somu's mother, Sujata had remained imprisoned within a private grief.

It was after hearing Somu's mother's uninhibited, heart-rending lamentation, her talk of the boys, that Sujata realized that Brati had not after all abandoned her to the desolation of a private grief. He had bound her to others like her, given her a new family.

But how could Sujata find her liberation in the midst of all those people? She was rich and belonged to another class. Why should they accept her as one of them?

Somu's mother said, Laltu went around desperately looking for a job. He didn't get one. That's what hit him. And a rage swelled within him.

This time too Somu's mother wept. Sujata stroked her arm.

In a year the house had become more ramshackle, it bore its poverty more blatantly. Somu's mother must have been wearing a sari that she could not wear before a visitor. At Sujata's arrival she had gone in to change into a more presentable one. The one she now wore was in such tatters, patched and worn, what could she have been wearing before?

Sujata could see that the thatched roof had come down on one side and had to be supported with a stick. The low bedstead was no longer there. Bricks on the floor supported a flat wooden plank instead. Cooking was probably no longer possible in the verandah. In a corner of the room one could see the small clay oven, a pan and a few utensils.

Somu's mother looked paler and more crushed. She looked like someone who had surrendered to destiny in sheer despair. Her appearance carried the look of death that one saw occasionally in an abandoned child on a city pavement, a kitten in the gutter, or a scrawny little crow.

But Somu's elder sister looked more determined, arrogant, angry. In the past year she must have had to fight tooth and nail, and the struggle must have left her seared and corroded. Sujata gazed hungrily, thirstily, at Somu's mother, at their room. Her mind went on warning her that she would never come here again. She would never again sit before Somu's mother and feel that she was not alone. What would Sujata be doing on the next seventeenth of January? From the last seventeenth of January to this, she knew that she had a place where she could go and sit for a while and have company. But it did not escape her that Somu's sister had spurned her and walked out. Her attitude conveyed to Sujata that she was unwanted here.

That was why she gazed around the room and at Somu's mother so avidly. This was the room where Brati had spent the last few hours of his life, he had lain there on the plain mattress laid out by Somu's mother. Somu's mother had had Sujata's son with her till a few minutes before his death.

Somu's mother had said, You've felt the pain, and that's why you come. As for me, Didi, I have eyes, yet I'm blind, I have legs yet I'm lame. Didi, my daughter tells me she'll never get a job because she's Somu's sister. Can it be true, Didi?

How would Sujata know what's true and what's not true? Those who defied the system were no longer living. But their families remained. There was an unwritten but ruthlessly effective policy for them. Was there a similar unwritten policy for their families too?

There was an unwritten policy of silence for two and a half years, right through the period when Baranagar and Kashipur were purged of the enemies of society. There was a premeditated policy behind the whole sequence of national events, the elephant cubs airlifted to Tokyo, the film festival at Metro, the writers and artists who addressed the meeting on the Maidan, and the fortnight of celebrations at the Rabindra Sadan dedicated to the great poet.

There was really nothing to get disturbed about, since nothing really important had happened. Did it matter, after all, if a few thousands of young men were no more? Sujata did not know what the other mothers thought, but she had felt then as she felt now that it was only in West Bengal that the youth felt hounded, threatened, on the verge of death. But of course more important events must have taken place elsewhere. The nation, the state, refused to acknowledge their existence, their passion, their indomitable faith in the teeth of death, all that they stood for.

What terrified Sujata was that nobody found it abnormal that everyone in the state should deny them and join in a conspiracy of pretence, the pretence of normalcy. Sujata had felt in the marrow of her bones how terrifying, brutal and violent this normalcy was. While the Bratis were being killed in the prisons and on the streets, chased relentlessly by the black vans, and being torn to pieces by frenzied mobs, the conscience-keepers of society had not a word to say about them. They all maintained their silence on this one issue.

Sujata found this pretence of normality ominously frightening. She was terrified when she saw how these silent witnesses were so complacent in their presumption that they were all normal, conscientious and magnanimous individuals. While their benevolence extended to the rest of the world, nearer home their outlook became opaque, hazy, unclear.

Deny the existence of a few thousands of the country's youth. Deny them altogether—that would be enough to wipe them out. The prisons are overflowing. There's no information about thousands of the country's young men. Ignore them. That's the way to exterminate them.

But their families? Is there a policy to exterminate them too, by denying them?

Sujata did not know what to say. All that she could say was—But I'm working still.

Don't compare yourself and my daughter, Didi. With all the contacts you have! Didn't you notice how all their names appeared in the papers, but Brati's name never appeared? Didi, I have no contacts, I don't have the money to hush things up or get things done.

Sujata knew that Somu's mother would feel the difference. A terrible, shocking pain had brought them together at Kantapukur and at the crematorium, but it was an affinity that could not last. Time was stronger than grief. Grief is the bank, Time the flowing river, heaping earth upon earth on grief.

Then a time comes when nature, with its ruthless logic, throws up new shoots out of the grief submerged under the alluvium of time.

Shoots of hope, sorrow, thought and hate.

The shoots grow till they snatch at the sky.

Time works wonders. Sujata was struck with fear whenever she thought of the omnipotence of time. There may even come a time when Brati's face would be a faint dab in Sujata's awareness, like a faded, old photograph. Some day maybe Sujata would mention Brati casually to anybody and everybody, and shed tears openly.

Time can do anything. Two years ago grief had made her and Somu's mother one. And it was time again that had wiped out the equation. The sharp assault of grief had wiped away the class distinctions that normally separated them.

But time had restored the class distinctions with the passage of time.

Sujata asked, Didn't Samiran's[17] sister pass some examination?

She sat for her First Part. She would have been a graduate if she could have appeared for her Second Part. But now she's learning typing. Every other day she's loath to go. She grumbles, I don't have proper clothes, I don't have money to buy a pair of slippers, I won't go. She says, I won't let my life go to waste like this, all for you. She speaks in a temper, but, Didi, she'd never forsake her obligations.

I don't think she'll have any problems because of Samiran. Still, I'll be on the lookout for a job for her.

What do you know, Didi? She lost a good tuition the other day. She used to get forty rupees. The boy's father told her, no, I can't keep you on. Your brother belonged to the Party. That's the truth, Didi.

They can't all be the same.

It's up to you, Didi. But she's done a good thing. She has sent the youngest two to a government boarding school. When children don't have a father, they put them into the orphanage.

That was a good thing to do.

My daughter tells me, Didi, people in the colony ask her why Brati's mother visits us. One of the gang that killed our boys asked her, are the mothers, Brati's and yours, ganging up? Why would an elephant step into a mole's hole? My daughter is scared. She comes home late in the evening after her tuitions, she has to do the marketing. She is scared of them. They are capable of anything.

They? Who are they?

Yes, Didi. The same ones. They have all changed to the other Party. They were never punished. They go about, their heads held high. They tell my daughter, Hey, why didn't you have the last rites for your brother? It would've been a great feast for us. They're fiends, Didi. They are always there at the tea shop.

It now struck Sujata that every time she had come, she had left the taxi at the crossing and made it to their house in a cycle rickshaw, she had never looked to the left or to the right. It had never struck her that Brati's killers could be sitting there all the time at the tea shop. It had never struck her that they could move about freely, could taunt Somu's sister so mercilessly, and could even break into guffaws of obscene laughter. What a city to live in, she thought, where such horrors could take place, and the routine of cultural festivals and fairs dedicated to the poet Tagore could continue unaffected.

The killers were safe once they changed their Party affiliations and the banners they carried. And yet the prison walls rose higher, and watchtowers loomed over the walls. All these things were happening together, but for how long?

Somu's mother said, You are fortunate, Didi. When you have another son, you can console yourself with him. Hold him tight to you and forget your dead son, Didi. I have lost one of my ribs. The pyre that burns in my heart will burn till I mount the pyre myself.

Sujata wanted to tell Somu's mother that if she too could have cried aloud and lamented like her, it would have saved her. But if she told Somu's mother that she had to bear within herself the burden of her grief for Brati like an inert rock, that she had never been able to weep for him, then Somu's mother would think her unnatural. She could not weep before those whose first concern at Brati's death had been to seek a way to hush up the news; her throat closed up tight. Somu's mother would not understand.

For Somu's father and mother had not thought of such things at the time.

It was still before midnight . . . a nightmare, the whole thing was like a nightmare . . . it had not turned midnight yet when they had encircled Somu's house. As they gathered one by one, Somu's mother saw them and leapt up, a hand clamped to her mouth. Somu's father said in utter helplessness, What shall we do now? Let's see if we can escape through the back door.

Somu said softly, It's no use, Baba. They've surrounded the other side too. I can hear them.

A hard cold voice hissed, Send them out to us.

Somu's father said, Isn't that Babu's voice?

The fierce voice again, Send them out. Or we'll set the house on fire. Come out, Somu. If you're your father's son, come out!

Somu turned to the rest of his group—If I go out first, they'll take me first. Won't you, at least one of you, be able to make your escape?

Come on out!

Brati had told Somu, It's no use, Somu. Why should you go alone? We'll go out together.

A nightmare . . . a nightmare still.

Brati was the first to get up. He walked up to the window and called out, Stop shouting. We're coming out. Wait for us.

The bastard's got a flunkey with him. It's one of those Calcutta boys. Come out, you son of a bitch!

No Somu, don't go out! Somu *re*! Somu-u-u-u!

Don't cry, Ma. Baba, take care of ma. We are going out. Or they'll set the house on fire.

Bijit had tied his pyjama cords tight, smoothened his hair. Partha was the quietest of them all. It was Partha who gave the first order—Let's go, Bijit.

Bijit and Partha had flick-knives with them, Somu and Brati were unarmed. They stood up, linked hands and raised their slogans as they opened the door.

Somu's father made an attempt to step before them—I'll die before they get you. But Somu pushed him aside, shouting slogans they stepped out, darkness outside, a crowd of pitch-dark faces, loud laughter and yells, cries scattering the laughter all around, lights going off one by one in the neighbouring houses, doors and shutters slamming shut, scared faces drawing back, over there wolf whistles flung at the sky, rending the sky, as when Durga images are toppled over into the dark river, while slogans rose from their throats. Bijit and Partha rushed straight at them, gripping their knives firmly, a voice—They're attacking! A scream—Bastards, you dare flaunt knives!? Another voice—Kill the bastards! Three voices still shouting slogans, someone has already skillfully manoeuvred a noose around Bijit's throat and strangled him. Slogans still. Slogans. Slogans. Zindabad! Long Live—! Long live! Wild confusion. The slogans stop abruptly. The killers leave. Staccato sound of shots. Stench of gunpowder on the still winter air—the stink of gunpowder—the dark faces receding—Somu's father broke into a loud wail, beating his chest, as he fell down—Somu! Dada! The sisters screamed. Somu's mother knew no more. Unconscious. Darkness. Darkness, darkness, darkness.

How could Somu's mother ever understand why Sujata could not weep? How could she believe that they tried not to mention Brati in that house? How could she see the point of Brati's father running around to ensure that Brati's name did not appear in the Press?

Somu's father had never thought of saving his skin, never thought such behaviour possible. Somu's father—the poor shopkeeper who had no capital!—had never come to know the kind of people who could think in such ways. The two fathers, Somu's and Brati's, lived in the same country, but poles apart.

Somu's father had hoped that once he approached the police, all would be taken care of. The killers would get scared and run away. Hurrying, panting, he somehow managed to rush to the police station. At that time lights shone day and night in the police stations. Please, Sir, please come! If you come right now my son may live! Maybe I could take him to hospital. I touch your feet, Sir!

The officer, though young, was experienced beyond his years. When Somu's father began to name the killers, he yelled at him. Somu's father was a helpless creature, like a worm anybody could crush beneath their feet. Fear silenced him for a while but then he began to insist again— I've seen them with my own eyes. I've heard their voices.— No, you haven't heard their voices—Please come, Sir—Yes,

yes, the van will go. At this point Somu's father had recognized another police officer and pleaded with him too, falling at his feet. At some point the van came. Somu's father climbed in. As the van entered the colony, he cried, like a madman, gasping and panting—Somu, answer me, my son! Somu *re*!—Strange, the van needed no directions. It made straight to the football ground. As the lights of the van hit the spot, some figures ran away. When the lights began to catch the faces, the van slowed down deliberately. By the time the van reached the spot, they had all had time to escape. When the van stopped, its lights were trained on Bijit. As the beam touched a body, Somu's father shrieked. Even as he called out—Somu!—he fell unconscious. He could see them dragging Somu by his feet and shoving him into the maws of the hungry van. It swallowed him up. Somu's head struck against something. Somu's father made an attempt to say—Watch his head!—But he could not utter the words. It was quarter past three. The van had never come so promptly before.

He went back to the police station after it was over. He wanted to record his deposition. He even complained to Lalbazaar, the Police Headquarters, against the local officer. It was all useless. Crying—O God! There's no justice in this country!—he fell and wounded his head on the pavement. His brother-in-law's son had to help him home.

How could Somu's mother understand Sujata? If Sujata tried to explain to her that it was Brati, Brati alone of all her children, who laid his head on her lap and fell asleep, placed his head on her shoulder while speaking to her, saying, Ma, won't you soap my back for me? Hem has again brought me cold tea; we'll go to the cinema together this evening, Ma, when you come back from the bank; I have to return these notes today, you must copy them out for me. Somu's mother would not find anything exceptional in it, for that is how all sons she knew behaved with their mothers.

If Sujata had told her that she lived in a shiftless, rootless, lifeless society where the naked body caused no embarrassment, but natural emotions did; if she had told her that mothers and sons, fathers and sons, husbands and wives never hit one another even when relationships stood irremediably poisoned, never wept aloud, showed their best manners to everyone, Somu's mother would not have been able to make any sense of it at all. The language would be Bengali, but the sense of the words would escape Somu's mother.

If Sujata told her that she came here to know Brati, her dead son, better, Somu's mother would not understand. If Sujata had told her that when Brati began to change it was not due only to books or political lectures; that Brati had felt the anguish of men like Somu, son of poor parents, or those like Laltu, humiliated by fate and life, and other men like them, as keenly as if it was his own, and that had caused him to change. Life itself had forced him to change. He gave up the life he was born to. If he had stuck to it, Brati would have gone to Britain, returned from Britain, found a good job, and risen up the social ladder with ease.

But Somu's mother would not have understood any of this. She said, Your son's face moves in my mind, Didi. Those who have nothing go crazy. Even as a boy Somu would say, Are we beggars? Why must we beg for things that should be ours by right, and get kicked in return? But Brati had everything, Didi. Why did he come here to die?

He had come to warn them.

You knew the course your son had chosen. Why didn't you warn him?

Somu's mother did not know that she had scored over Sujata; she had known what Somu was up to. Sujata may have had an aristocratic bearing, a stiff upper lip, a watch on her wrist and an expensive handloom sari. But Somu's mother did not know that Sujata as a mother had lost out to several thousands of mothers, for she had never known what Brati was up to.

Whether in triumph or in humiliation, Sujata could never lie.

Brati knew that.

Sujata said, I didn't know.

If you had known, Didi! Would a mother ever send her son to his death?

Sujata stood up.

Come again, Didi. Talking to you brings me peace.

Sujata knew that she would never come there again.

I'm going.

Sujata all of a sudden put her hand on Somu's mother's shoulder. She said, I'll always remain grateful to you.

What's there to be grateful for! Those who suffer understand suffering.

At this moment of final parting, Sujata felt the urge to give Somu's mother something really precious. She felt the desire to draw something out of the prison that she had carved within herself, out of her own grief, and offer it to Somu's mother. And so, the one thing that she could not bring herself to say, she put into words for the first time— It was Brati's birthday the day after they were killed. On the seventeenth, Brati would have turned twenty, and entered his twenty-first year.

Late Afternoon

It was a house quite close to her own. Sujata had often glanced at it while passing, but she had never entered it, and didn't know who owned it. An old-fashioned two-storeyed building, with a verandah running in front. The top of the house was obviously designed after the marquee of the old Metro cinema in Calcutta. It bore a tablet—Purva Ganga Nagar—probably the name of the original owner's home village. In the last twenty years, Sujata had watched the house change till it looked like the city itself—a portion of it sparklingly new, flushed with its coat of enamelled paint, air-coolers under the windows, the rest shabby, with peeling plaster, and windows covered with filthy curtains made from tattered saris. The ground floor facing the street was rented out to a number of single-room establishments—a laundry, a dispensary for homeopathic drugs, a shop that repaired radio sets. Obviously wealth and poverty were distributed between the claimants.

A dark passage led past the common courtyard to the large room towards the rear of the house. A custard apple tree stood abandoned and desolate before it. The walls and the ceiling had lost their plaster, the floor was worn to the underlying layer of bricks. A large, low, flat bed covered a part of the room. There were dusty, unused law books in the cupboard, which was rusted at the bottom. Sujata sat on the bed. Nandini sat on a cane stool facing her.

Anindya betrayed us.

Nandini repeated the words. She had said the words once already, and just as before, when she spoke the words again, her eyes betrayed a flicker of disbelief like the shadow of a fleeting cloud. As if she found it hard to accept, or couldn't understand, how Anindya could do it knowing full well that his betrayal would spell death for Somu and all the others.

I don't know the whole story, Nandini.

I know. You people never know anything. For people like you, these are just stray episodes. But now you know that it's wrong to carry on presuming that one needn't know why and how such things happen.

Anindya betrayed us. Brati, like a fool, had trusted Anindya. For Anindya was Nitu's recruit, and Nitu was Brati's friend.

A person recruited by Nitu was above suspicion, because Nitu was Brati's friend and comrade. But had Nitu known everything about Anindya before bringing him into the organization? Sujata thought to herself.

A long spell in the solitary cell in prison made one perhaps oversensitive. For a solitary cell is too lonely, too desolate. There one lived all alone with oneself within four walls, with an iron door and a sole small hole in the wall. Immured in the solitary cell one tried to penetrate the world outside with a mind as keen and cutting as the knife of the surgeon in the morgue or the blade of a bayonet, to discover those that remembered. Occasionally the doors opened. They were taken not to the world they yearned for, but to a room of a different kind. Soundproof. The doors and windows lined with hollow rubber tubes covered with soft felt. The groans that arose from the room, the screams, the sound of beating and thrashing, the grating voice of the interrogation, the rubber tubes held all the sounds within check and confined them to the room. A thousand-watt lamp glared at the naked eyes of the person being held in that room. The person in charge sat in the dark. Smoker or not, a cigarette glowed between his fingers. From time to time, the interrogator, educated and sophisticated, could ask a civil and harmless question like 'Oh, so you're Chatterjee's friend?' and clamp the burning cigarette to the skin of the face naked under the thousand-watt lamp. Cigarette burns caused only surface cutaneous injury. Only the skin gets charred. The burn could always be cured with an ointment. It is described as 'surface cutaneous healing'. The burn on the skin healed soon. But in the young heart within, every single burn ached for ever. Then back to the solitary cell. Alone with oneself.

The mind and the senses grew hypersensitive in that living with oneself, keen and sharp and cutting like the knife of the surgeon in the morgue or the blade of a bayonet. So Nandini could sense the mute question that rose within Sujata—Did Nitu know when he brought Anindya in?

Nandini said, We'll never know whether or not Nitu knew what Anindya was up to. Do you know what happened to Nitu?

No.

Nitu had several aliases. Many names. There was a massive round-up after Brati and their group had left. In his own locality they all knew him as Dipu. Nitu decided to run away at that time. He moved to the industrial belt, not too far away from his own place. There the local police arrested him, thinking he was someone else. Just then the OC of the police station in his own locality turned up there. He had no business to be there, really, at that time. But the newspapers were also betraying us. Every now and then they would print information about our hideouts, the places where we had our hospitals, about our work in the villages. Writing articles about us. One of these had given him a clue, and that is why the OC was there, in the industrial belt. He stopped his jeep and came in to have a cup of tea. And collect some gur.

Some gur?

Yes, the sugarcane gur there is famous. They had bought two pots of it for him. He came in and spotted Nitu. He asked, Dipu? You here? After hours of interrogation and being beaten badly, Nitu was extremely nervous, and without a thought he said, Yes. I don't know why they've dragged me here. The OC immediately made him sit in his jeep. On the way he fed him at a restaurant, offered him a cigarette. Since Nitu was very popular in his area, and had never been involved in any action there, he still hoped to get out of it somehow.

Couldn't he?

No. They brought him back to his own locality, and then beat him to death right before the police station. The women of the locality gathered there later to register their protest; even they were teargassed.

It never appeared in the papers.

No.

Then?

So, Nitu is dead. We'll never know whether he knew Anindya's intentions. Still I feel . . . What do you feel?

One should have known.

Who? Nitu?

Sujata had never known Nitu, yet she could utter the name with easy familiarity, as if Brati had drawn her into a relationship with all of them.

Yes, Nitu, Brati and me.

What should you have known?

That just as we had a programme, so the others too had a programme.

What programme?

A programme of betrayal, of course.

Nandini spoke in a calm, cold and almost indifferent voice. Sujata realized that the fleeting surprise in her eyes when she had named Anindya was not so much at Anindya's betrayal as at themselves. They had developed a burning faith in the faithlessness of everything that spelt Establishment, and yet had never thought that there could be people who could pose as friends, write about them in the Press and take part in a deliberate programme to betray them.

Now everything seems to have been a part of the betrayal.

Nandini spoke again. On her thin, dark and weary face Sujata could see a permanent shadow under her eyes. Just as shadows linger on the slopes of hills or the foothills. Some unknown land of eternal shadows in the foothills.

It felt as if Nandini could never be known or understood. She had a sudden feeling of irreparable loss, of a void. It grieved Sujata that she would never know the girl Brati loved, that Nandini's mind would remain unknown to her for ever. Pain. She would never be able to go to Somu's mother again. She would never know Nandini well. Deep pain and a sense of loss. Sujata had never shared in any of Nandini's beliefs or experiences, she had never tried to know what the Bratis and the Nandinis felt. Who can tell her how worthy or useless all the things were which had kept her so preoccupied? Was this why Brati left home that evening in his blue shirt—so that Sujata would recognize the defaults in her nature and in her mind? Was that why he had stopped at the foot of the stairs and looked back up at her?

If Sujata got that moment back again she would rush down the stairs, and hug him hard, body of her body. She would tell him, Brati, I have to know everything, I'll begin to know everything. Just don't go out, Brati, please don't. In Calcutta a young man of twenty cannot go from one part of the city to another safely. Don't go, please.

But time past is time lost. Time is a ruthless killer, as cruel as destiny. Time is the river Ganga, with grief for its banks. The tide of time carries alluvium in to cover up grief. And then fresh sprouts of greenery break through, reaching fingers to the sky, young shoots of hope and pain and joy and ecstasy.

Everything, everyone, seems part of the betrayal.

From across the wall of Sujata's thoughts, Nandini spoke.

Don't, Nandini. It'll bring you more unhappiness.

No, no. When I didn't know of the betrayal, I had tremendous self-confidence. But that confidence was unfounded. Still, when I started doubting, when I thought and thought over the facts, I began to feel much more sure. Now I know where I stand.

Does it help you any?

Yes. Now when I think back, how naively we had assumed that an era was coming to an end. You're bringing in a new age. Brati and I would walk all the way from Shyambazar to Bhowanipur, just talking all the way. Whatever we saw on the way—the people, the houses, the neon signs, red roses in a wayside florist's stall, festoons on the streets, newspapers pasted on boards near the bus stops, smiling faces, a beautiful image in a poem in a little magazine picked up at one of the stalls on the way, crowds clapping like mad at a political rally on the Maidan, snatches of lilting tunes from Hindi films—everything spelt ecstasy; we couldn't hold in the joy, we felt explosive. Felt loyal to all and everything. I'll never feel the same way again. It will never come back. Total loss. An era is really over for good. The person I was then is dead.

Why, Nandini? Because Brati is dead?

Because Brati is dead. And so many things are dead too. I too have died a slow death as I thought and thought over the past all by myself in a solitary cell.

Don't talk like that, please.

You talk like my mother. She doesn't understand, nor will you.

But can't I understand at all, Nandini?

How can you? Did any of you ever take a personal loyalty pledge like we did? To everything of everyday life?

No. Sujata had not. She had not pledged her loyalty to the smile of a stranger on the street, to the snatch of a tune floating in the air, to red roses, to the bright street lights, to the hanging festoons across the streets. Where had Sujata pledged her faith? To which things?

Now I know how betrayal worked, how it works even now.

Even now, Nandini?

Sure. How else can one explain the walls raised higher around the prisons, the watchtowers? Why doesn't a single person raise his voice when thousands of young men are still rotting in the prisons? And when they do, they keep the interests of their own political party in mind? How is it that we who would like to carry on, cannot print a single bulletin? Why are we denied the simple facilities of a printing press and newsprint, while innumerable journals come out, continue to come out, and one hears that they are all sympathetic to the cause? Betrayal. There are all those who talk for the sake of talking, never realizing even that in the process they are betraying us. Why do these poets have to cry their hearts out over Bangladesh in the Seventies and go on churning out poems dripping with sentiment? Betrayal. Why do the round-ups continue? The firings within the prisons? The arrests? Betrayal.

Still?

Yes, even now. Do you think there are no arrests because the newspapers don't write about them? Have the shootings stopped? Has anything stopped? Why should it stop? What has ended? Nothing. Nothing has ended. Only a generation between sixteen and twenty-four was wiped out. Is being wiped out . . .

Suddenly, impulsively, Sujata did something she never did. It was not like her to act on emotion alone. She had never in her life dared to surrender to her normal impulses. When she was younger, Dibyanath would reprimand her if she ran to the window to watch a gathering storm. The lessons forcibly learnt in the tender years of life remain insurmountable. Yet Sujata allowed herself to touch Nandini's hand. Even as she did, she knew it was a moment, an opportunity that she would never know again. Time was the arch fugitive, always on the run. She would never be able to retrieve the moment when Brati in his blue shirt stood at the foot of the stairs and looked up at her. She could feel within herself, deep within her mind, a limitless void, an inconsolable grief, because she knew she would never have Nandini so close to her again.

So Sujata placed her hand on Nandini's. Would she push her hand away and force her back to the barren existence that was her life? Would Nandini's eyes bear the same rejection that she had seen in Somu's sister's? The very thought chilled Sujata. Sujata could well envisage the solitary cell that her existence would be from now on, with Dibyanath, Jyoti, Neepa, Tuli, Bini and the colleagues in the bank; all outside; and within, Brati, only Brati, but why just Brati, also Somu's mother, Nandini, the grief of separation from everyone of them held within her. From now on she would be alone, totally alone. No one would again throw open the doors of her solitary cell, to bring her out and ask—Are you Brati Chatterjee's mother?

But Nandini did not push her hand away.

For a while she remained silent and motionless. Then, with fingers shy and hesitant and reluctant, she caressed Sujata's hand. Sujata drew her hand away. She was grateful, ever so grateful, that Nandini had actually placed her hands upon Sujata's.

I loved Brati.

Brati had told me about you.

Did he?

Yes. On the sixteenth of January.

Strange!

What's strange?

Didn't he tell you earlier?

No.

I knew that if he told anyone, Brati would tell you. For he didn't have faith in anyone else in that house.

Brati?

Why are you surprised?

Brati wasn't close to the others. Still . . .

What is there to be surprised about? Does one have to love and trust others only because they happen to be one's father or sister or brother, even if there's no gesture of love from them?

I wouldn't know, Nandini. I've just begun to realize how little I knew Brati. I didn't know then.

Did you ever try to know him?

Sujata shook her head. She had never been able to lie. Brati knew that.

That's the way your generation is. You ask for every-thing—love, loyalty, obedience. But why do you demand it? How can you?

Shouldn't we, Nandini?

No. You shouldn't. Many of you have forfeited the right to expect it! There were others, of course, who had a different relationship with their parents. Antu, Dipu, Sanchayan, all had happy lives. And yet they too joined the movement. How did they? Who can say?

You explain it, Nandini.

Take Brati. He could never communicate with his father. At a time when the first gesture should have come from his father, his father never tried to build up a relationship with him. Brati used to say that his father used you like a doormat.

Did Brati say that?

How else would I know?

Brati said that!

Sujata's face flushed red, then regained its normal look. So Brati had known it all the time. And had tried to protect his mother with his love. Once, when he was only six, he had found his mother weeping silently, and told her, Ma, I'll buy you a sari printed with tigers and hunters.

He told me that his father bribed clients away from other firms. He was one CA whose death wouldn't be mourned by anyone. With a wife like you and four grown-up children, he was a great womanizer . . . he had set up some typist in a rented flat. Brati had threatened him once over that, did you know that?

When?

In November. Two months before he was killed.

Now for the first time it was clear to Sujata why Brati, in the last few months of his life, had avoided seeing or talking to Dibyanath. And why Dibyanath had never uttered Brati's name. He had never even repeated the old joke: Your youngest son . . . does he too live in our house?

Brati's brother and sisters admired their father. Brati used to say that they were not human. His eldest sister was a nympho, the other sister a bundle of complexes, impossible to understand, his brother a pimp. That was how he described them. Only you . . . he loved you. That is why he hadn't left home.

Where would he have gone?

He was not supposed to stay at home any longer. I think he was postponing his departure only because of you. But finally, on the nineteenth of January we were to leave Calcutta, he and I and several others.

Where to?

To the base.

Brati would have left his home?

Had he been alive he would have. If Anindya hadn't betrayed us, he would have. For Brati and those like him, distrust begins at home. Then . . .

Somu's father was not like Brati's . . .

For Somu and his kind, distrust begins the other way round. In his moments of anger, Somu would say that he would kill his father first, for taking everything lying down. He was bullied by everyone from the fishseller to the local tough. They bought things from him and would never pay. Antu, Dipu and Sanchayan, on the other hand, respected their fathers. One can't totally explain them. It's all so puzzling!

What else did Brati say about me?

Many, many things. Not all the time, but from time to time. See, Brati was to leave for the base on the fifteenth. But he postponed it to the nineteenth. Only I knew about his birthday, that his birthday was very special for you. He did not believe in ceremonies. Still, only for you he went on putting it off . . . I knew, but didn't tell anyone. I scolded Brati, though.

What did he say?

He smiled. The way he would smile whenever he wanted to parry a question. Then he said, Perhaps I'm not as strong as you are.

What else did Brati say?

He said you were a good person. You were thoroughly non-understanding, but he could explain to you. He had no resentment against you. When he won the National Scholarship he thought for a time in terms of a good job. He planned to take you away somewhere. But then of course he dropped the idea.

Was Sujata's hungry, clinging love then indirectly responsible for Brati's death? Brati had stayed on in Calcutta on that fateful day only to avoid hurting her. Otherwise he would have left for the base. Where was the base?

A long sojourn in the solitary cell gave one's mind a probing sharpness. Like the knife of the surgeon in the morgue.

Nandini said, Don't blame yourself alone. For all you know, he might have been killed at the base itself. Though, if Anindya had not betrayed . . .

Yet one feels . . .

Anindya's betrayal is the main thing. We hadn't joined the party as dissidents from some other party. We were direct converts. But Anindya had broken away from his old party. He had come with definite instructions. The original plan was that Somu and the others would return to the colony. But then the decision was changed. We have suffered too often for such organizational lapses. In an underground organization you always depend on others. Anindya was to inform Somu and his group not to return to the colony, and then he was supposed to inform Brati that he had passed on the message.

So that is why Brati was waiting at home.

Yes. But Anindya never told Somu and his group anything. Instead, he went off to the colony and told the others. He never returned. He left Calcutta at once. I was supposed to meet Laltu in the evening. When I found out that they had gone back, I informed Brati. Brati didn't wait for any further directions. He rushed off to warn Somu and his group.

How . . . how did you learn . . . ?

I came to know early the next morning. Partha's brother had managed to escape that night. He told me.

And you . . .

I was arrested the same morning.

That morning itself!

Yes. Anindya betrayed our whole unit.

Where is he now?

Who? Anindya? Anindya is not in Calcutta.

Where is he?

In another state.

Then what happened?

I was in prison. At that time I thought . . .

What did you think?

I thought of killing Anindya. I don't any longer.

What do you think now?

No, Mashima,[18] I haven't changed. It's not just against Anindya, we probably have to fight in other ways against everything.

Again, Nandini?

Why not?

Tell me why. If you do that, you too . . .

You don't understand. You love too intensely . . . and then the prison, the interrogation, the lamp burning your eyes—they try to break you—then you find yourself. I'll never be able to be simple or normal again, in the way you're thinking of. Not just because of Brati. If Brati had been alive, we might have got married, or we might not. What we might have done depended on so many other factors. I do not know what might have happened. I won't tell you the rest but . . . you lose the taste for so many things.

You loved Brati very much, didn't you?

That's what I thought then. I still do. They say one forgets with time. Or that his face will grow hazy in my mind. I'm scared when I think of it.

I know.

You too?

Yes.

I don't know whether or not I'll forget him. I don't know whether or not he'll fade from my memory. But it's not Brati alone. When I think, so many died, for what? Do you know what hurt me most when I came out of prison?

What?

When I saw how everything looked normal, wonderful, and there was the general feeling that the dark days were over, that everything had quietened down. That broke my heart.

But haven't things quietened down?

No! Nandini screamed, leaving Sujata stunned.

Nothing has quietened down, it can't! It wasn't quiet then, it isn't now. Don't say that it has all cooled down. After all you are Brati's mother. You of all persons should never say or believe that all is quiet now. Where does such complacency come from?

Has nothing changed? No. Nothing has. Why did they die? What has changed? Are men now all happy? Have the political games ended? Is it a better world?

No.

Thousands of young men still languish in the prisons without trial. And you can say it's quiet now?

Nandini shook her head over and over again. Then she said, That's what people try to tell me. My mother tells me, since you won't do anything else, why don't you marry and raise a family?

Are you . . . ?

Medical grounds. Otherwise they wouldn't have let me out. I didn't want to die. If I hadn't been let out, I wouldn't have got the medical treatment that I needed. Even now I'm interned.

Treatment for what?

Oh, so you haven't guessed! My optical nerves were damaged from the exposure to the glare of the lamp for forty-eight, seventy-two hours at a stretch. My right eye is totally blind. One can't tell by looking at me, though.

Well, I didn't.

I have lost an eye.

What will you do now?

I don't know. I know that I must have my eyes treated. But I don't know what else I'll do. I know also that I won't marry Sandip to please my mother.

Who is Sandip?

A young man with a good job. Perhaps it's fashionable now to marry women like us, as fashionable as the kind of poetry Dhiman Roy writes about us! For otherwise I don't have a clue as to why he should want to marry me.

What will you do, Nandini?

I've told you I don't know. I still feel disturbed and confused about so many things. Everything seems so strange, so unreal. I can't identify with anything. My experiences over the last few years have made me unfit for this so-called normalcy. All that you people find normal, I find abnormal. Can you tell me what I should do?

I can't.

Almost none of my friends are alive. All the things I want to say, the people I want to talk about, all that my mind is full of, I can't speak of to anyone. There is no one I can talk to.

You have your parents at home, your family?

Yes. This is not my home. It belongs to a relation. My parents don't live in Calcutta.

If you stayed with them . . .

To them too I am a problem, I know that. I don't know what I should do. Some day you might hear . . .

What?

Nandini smiled. A bright, dazzling smile. She said, You might hear that they have arrested me again. Who knows.

Sujata still waited. Time was running out. It was getting dark. Winter evenings come early. It was time for her to go back home, but her feet refused to obey her.

Shouldn't you be going?

Yes, I should.

We won't be meeting again.

Are you going away somewhere?

No, I'll be staying here. But what is the point of meeting again?

Sujata shook her head. She knew there was no point really. For their lives moved along parallel lines, with no meeting point.

May I give you something?

What?

This is for you to keep.

It was a portrait of Brati. It was always with her, in her bag.

Nandini took the portrait. Placed it on the ledge. Then she said, I don't have one with me any longer. I used to have one.

I have others. It must have been taken by someone in college.

I know. It was Anindya.

I have to leave now, Nandini. Please keep well. Please get in touch if you need anything, anything at all.

I shall.

She smiled when she said it. But Sujata knew that Nandini would never get in touch. Nandini knew she would not. They would turn into strangers again. But

Sujata's world would not be the same. Why Brati had left that evening in his blue shirt, how he had turned into a number, 1084—all day long Sujata had been finding bits and pieces of the explanation. She would spend the rest of her life piecing them together.

Let me come with you. There's no light outside.

Nandini groped her way to the door. As she watched her, Sujata thought that perhaps both her eyes were damaged.

Will you come out?

No, I'm not allowed to. Home interned. And I just can't make it by myself.

Then let it be.

Sujata stroked her face and forehead. She had an urge to hold her close and rock her gently. Just as she had held Brati close, she felt like holding Nandini. A normal, living, hungry desire. The same desire had made Somu's mother cry out in the crematorium, Let me hold him! I'll be quiet once I can hold him to my breast, I promise you. I won't cry again.

Brati and I had once walked right up to your place, busy talking. Brati had promised to take me to you one day. That was a long time ago.

Sujata shook her head. Not so long ago, Nandini.

Only four years or so if one counted days. But by a different count, it was now way back in the past. Countless light years had passed since those normal days when, at the end of a day, one could go and visit Brati's mother.

Sujata bid a soft goodbye. Nandini did not say a word. She turned back, supported herself against the grimy and dirty wall. She slowly started walking back. Each step she took carried her farther away from Sujata. Sujata came out onto the Calcutta streets again.

Evening

Winter evenings gather early. That's why it was already dark. The lighted rooms in Sujata's house gleamed brighter against the darkness. For the last few days, on coming back from the bank, Sujata had been cleaning the windowpanes with soapwater. That was why the windows held such a sparkle. It had rained a few days ago, and there had been a drizzle even the day before. The rains had drawn the flying insects, beating their wings against the panes, and circling the sphere of light. These things happen, have always happened. But all that is normal was now abnormal for Nandini, and would remain abnormal for ever. Nandini had a shawl wrapped around her shoulders. Brati loved to wrap himself in an old and shabby shawl in winter.

Dibyanath must have been pacing up and down before the door for quite some time, for at Sujata's appearance he dropped the soft and considerate manner he had maintained for the last two years, and broke into his old, loud tone—So you're finally back! Wonderful!

Sujata did not reply. She was trying to calculate the time when Brati must have confronted Dibyanath with the typist. Yes—it was from then on that Brati began to contribute his scholarship money to the household. It was only now that Sujata knew why Brati had not left home at the time. He had stayed home only for her sake. Brati, why didn't you tell me everything? Your love for me had changed so much! It was more like a father's for his small daughter.

Sujata crossed the passage and slowly entered the drawing room. Flowers in all the vases. Bright, bright lights. The roses a deep red. Ah, those who had pledged their faith in the red roses and the glowing lights had shifted their allegiance long ago. Yet the roses remained as red as ever, the lights as bright as ever—Betrayal! The roses and the lights too had betrayed Nandini and Brati. Sujata shook her head.

The large table had been dragged out onto the lower verandah. In his school days, often, on a rainy day, Brati would bring the table out for a table tennis match with his school pals. They had once held a ceremony for the birth anniversary of Tagore on the verandah. Bablu, one of Brati's friends, was highly precocious. As a boy he had written that Tagore was so poor that he had to give up his studies after he had completed class eight and had supported his family by writing poems. Brati had recited Tagore's poem 'The Young Hero'. Light years had passed since then.

A milk-white cover on the table. One of the legs of the table bore the dents left by Brati, who would kick it with his boots. Forks, spoons, napkins, wine glasses, water glasses, plates and coffee cups stood neatly arranged on the table. There was no trace of Brati in this, in any of this. In the house where Brati grew up, spent his life, it was so difficult to find traces of him anywhere. Sujata noticed the cups, red and gold cherry blossoms on a black surface. They were Neepa's. So she must have arrived.

She entered the dining room. On the dining table were boxes of sandesh, rasagollas in earthen bowls, yoghurt. The boxes of food carried the names of the restaurants they came from—Waldorf and Sabir. The food for today had been ordered from outside. The sideboard held containers of sauce, vinegar, mustard, salt, pepper and salad. Bini had sliced the green chillies and soaked them in vinegar in a glass bowl.

Hem!

Hem came running.

A glass of lemon juice, please.

Hem left. Dibyanath came in.

Dibyanath looked middle-aged, carnal and fleshy. It struck Sujata for the first time that there was something ugly and gross about his hair cropped so close and the glaze of cream on his face. She felt it was time for Dibyanath to give up wearing the embroidered kurtas and costly shawls he wore for special occasions. The shoes he wore had been bought for the occasion. Even the vest he wore was expensive, Sujata knew.

What could you be thinking of? Didn't you know there'd be fifty guests tonight?

Of course I knew.

What was the idea, then?

All the arrangements had been made. Neepa's already here. You were at home. When everything's organized, don't make a fuss.

Make a fuss? Do you know what you're saying?

If . . . you . . . don't leave . . . this room . . . at once, I'll . . . leave . . . this house . . . and never come back again.

Sujata spoke cuttingly, pausing before each word. She hates, detests the man. Dibyanath and the typist. Dibyanath and a distant cousin. Dibyanath and his cousin's wife.

For Dibyanath it was a slap on the face. In the thirty-four years of their married life, Sujata had never spoken to him in that tone.

Don't I have the right to ask you where you've been all day?

No.

What?

Two years ago, for thirty-two, I never asked you where you spent your evenings, or who accompanied you on your tours for the past ten years, or why you paid the house rent for your ex-typist. You are never to ask me a thing. Never.

God!

When I was younger, I didn't understand. Then your mother covered up your sins—yes, sins—and I didn't feel like raking things up. Then I had no interest to know. But I have never spent my time, like you, stealing away, slinking away from your home, from your family, the way you have done all your life. Would you like to hear more?

You . . . today . . .

Yes, why not? Why not today? Get out.

Who? Me?

Yes. Get out.

Her words hit him like a whiplash. Dibyanath went out tamely, wiping the nape of his neck.

Sujata would not stay here after tonight. She would no longer stay in a house where Brati was no more. If only she had had the strength to come out with the truth and challenge Dibyanath while Brati had still been alive! And leave the house forever with Brati! Even then she might not have been able to affect the course of events. But she might have come a little closer to Brati. And Brati would have died with the knowledge that Sujata was not all that submissive and unprotesting. Now Brati would never know.

Hem came in with the sherbet. Sujata gulped it down. She said, Get me some hot water Hem. I'll have a bath. Don't carry the water up. Nathu must be around.

Nathu has gone for ice next door.

Was there no ice in our fridge?

No. The mechanic was here. He said something was wrong with the fridge. It would cost sixty rupees to repair and would take time.

Forget about the hot water, then.

Have your bath later then.

Maybe later.

Did you have anything to eat during the day?

Didn't feel like it.

Will you go upstairs now?

Yes.

Want anything to eat?

No. When did Neepa come?

In the morning. She had her lunch here.

Did she bring her daughter with her?

No. She had some programme at school.

Who arranged the rooms?

Bini.

Who brought the crockery out?

Tuli, all by herself. She gave me a scolding after you had left. She said that I was useless, just sat and ate all day, that I sponged off you in Brati's name.

Why did she scold you?

Her bath water had got too hot. She had asked me to grind something for her to put on her face, and I had forgotten to grind it for her.

Then?

Then she started cleaning up the rooms. Bini said, Why didn't you ask me? Can't you leave it to somebody else for today, at least? And then they fought, the two of them. I couldn't follow, it was all in English.

Why were you eavesdropping?

What a thing to say! Me, eavesdropping! They were shouting and screaming so loudly that they could be heard on the street.

Then?

Then Tuli must have given Neepa a ring. For she came along and coaxed Bini, and then Bini finished the rooms. Then the three of them had a hearty lunch and chatted together. They were no longer glum. Then the three of them went out together to get their hair done. When they came back they were laughing.

Didn't Tuli's friend come to get her hair done?

No.

Okay, you may leave now,

Hem left the room. Sujata followed her out. She began climbing the stairs, holding on to the railings. Pain racked her. She was in terrible pain the day before Brati was born. Why did she not remember the other births she had laboured through? Why did she remember Brati's birth alone? Was it because Brati would remain forever close to her heart as a bitter pain? Brati stood right here at the foot of the stairs that day . . . her stomach contracted with pain. She had planned to have the operation after Tuli's wedding. Now she knew it would have to be earlier. It would be a relief if the rest of the day passed off smoothly. Then she could take care of the next day.

She had not wanted Tuli's engagement to be on this day. But nobody had cared to ask her opinion. Tony Kapadia's mother's guru, Swamiji, lived in America. He had fixed the date. Tony never went against his mother. She provided the finance for his business.

Dibyanath was pleased. Tony was as much a mother-worshipper as he was. Whatever his mother said, Tony said, 'Yes'. Even if Tony had not been a mother's boy he would still have been an excellent choice as far as Dibyanath was concerned. It was Tony who had brought Dibyanath the Shaw and Benson account. Dibyanath was soft on Tony. Also, Tuli was his favourite. Everything about Tuli, her features, her nature, reminded him of his mother.

Tuli was the first in the family to know about Dibyanath's mistress, the typist. But she had kept it a secret. She hadn't felt dislike or disgust for Dibyanath. In fact, it was Sujata who had been revolted by the audacity of a woman who would go as far as to ring up Dibyanath's home and leave the message—Tell him I'll go to the market this evening. It was Tuli who would take the message. Dibyanath must have told the woman to trust Tuli alone with messages.

Tuli would always give Dibyanath his messages. In fact she had become strangely possessive about her father at the time. It was under her supervision that Dibyanath would dress up for the evening. Tuli alone knew that Dibyanath met his girlfriend on Mondays, Wednesdays and Fridays. She would religiously run upstairs with his chicken salad and soup when he came back from the evening with his mistress. She drew a strange sense of gratification and pride out of this. Like her grandmother. She would often project her father as the model of the virile man, and proclaim that if one married, one should marry only a man like him. She would say, My elder brother is a coward. He's tied to his wife's apron strings.

Jyoti had learnt of Dibyanath's infidelity from someone related to his in-laws. There was a fracas in the house over this. It was Tuli again who had said, Dada, it's easy to condemn Baba. But people who seek such escape have some unhappiness in their lives. Like Baba does.

Thakuma[19] used to tell us that her husband never spent an evening at home. Was my grandfather a lesser man for that?

Brati had not said a thing. He would not eat at the same table as Tuli. He would not say a word as long as Tuli was around. Now it seemed that Brati had known the whole story all along. He must have thought that if Sujata, who should be the first to protest, could keep quiet, why should he talk? But something must have shaken his loyalty, for how else would he have decided to leave home? Now Sujata would never get a chance to tell Brati why she had not protested. Brati would never know now that Sujata had suffered all the indignities only for his sake, so that he could finish his studies and take up a job. She had had plans to leave home with Brati once Brati was settled. Would Brati have changed his course had he known her plans? No, he would not. That she knew, and that was why he was her favourite child. Even in his childhood Brati had become aware of Sujata's intense loneliness and would console her—Ma, I'm going to put you inside a glass house once I grow up. A house built of magic glass, Ma, where you can see everyone but no one can see you.

That was why, in class ten, when he had been asked to write an essay on 'My Favourite Person', he had written about his mother. That was Brati. The Brati who would be scared at the sight of blood when he cut his finger, and would at the same time endure the pain tight-lipped. Sujata had an intense desire to caress Brati's face with her fingers. She would have liked to shut her eyes and feel with her fingertips the curve of the nostrils, the scar on the eyebrow, the lines of his face for the last time, but there was no part of his face that was not mutilated. It was not enough just to kill. It was an inevitable part of the pattern of killing to prolong the process of killing and watch with demonic glee the death throes of the man dying.

One could kill and go unpunished, for the killers were extremely cunning. Can any society be in a more terrifying situation? Why is there no one to identify those who initiated the killers into killing the youth? How could they go unscathed? Why does it all still remain so baffling?

Are they still active today, powerfully active even now? Nandini had said that nothing was quiet. Sujata had heard how the process worked. The killers would first try to bribe them. Then they tortured them. Needles under the nails, thousand-watt lamps searing the eyes, the genitals smashed. Yet young men like Brati refused to submit, they still went on refusing. Then from J.C. to P.C., from jail custody to police custody. Then the file was closed. A full stop. Ajoy Dutt's mother had said, Now you can close the file on Habul Dutt too. Habul was his alias. They had told Sanjiban's sister, Want a photograph to show your mother? Come after a month. There are seventy-two shots in the reel. Your brother was number thirty. We'll finish the reel in a month, then we'll have it developed and printed.

Sujata climbed up the staircase, clutching at the banister. As a little boy Brati used to slide down the banister. Hem would chase him with a glass of milk and Brati would slide down. This chase-and-get-me game would go on between the two for some time. When grown up, Brati had gone up and down these stairs day after day, yet the house carried no trace of Brati; but Brati was still present elsewhere, in the red roses in pavement stalls, in the hanging festoons, the bright streetlights, in the laughter of men, in the face of Somu's mother, in the dark, lasting shadows under Nandini's eyes—Where would Sujata look for him? She was so tired, ready to drop. Would Sujata go on searching and searching and searching for him because he lay spread over so many places, in so many things?

She entered Tuli's room.

Tuli and Neepa wore the same dark blue Benarasi saris and stoles. They were gifts from Dibyanath to his two daughters and Bini, for this very special day. Three saris and three stoles must have cost more than nine hundred rupees. Nine hundred rupees could relieve a lot of distress for someone like Somu's mother.

Tuli and Neepa turned towards her. The mirror reflected the three of them. Sujata stared at her crumpled sari, exhausted face, dishevelled, greying hair. Tuli and

Neepa were daintily dressed and beautiful. Their faces should have looked content, but there were deep lines of peevishness and discontent on their faces.

Tuli, your ornaments.

Sujata undid the clasp of her bag, and poured the jewellery out on the bed. Then she picked up a few pieces to put back in her bag.

Why are you putting them back?

I've given you all that I've given Neepa and Bini.

See, Didi? Didn't I tell you?

Neepa spoke in a wheedling, soft, self-sacrificing voice, You can give those to Tuli, Ma. I promise I won't lay claim to them.

Where's the question of you claiming anything?

You've given Bini as well.

If Brati were alive, I'd have given them to Brati's wife. One of these is for Suman, another's for your daughter.

The rest?

That's for me to decide.

Tuli hissed venomously—Strange! You know how fond I am of antique jewellery. And you knew that Tony was planning to model costume jewellery on these for export.

You had said that, and I heard you. But now I've changed my mind.

But why?

Just like that. I've now given away all the jewellery that I got from your father and your grandmother. These were from my father, I'll keep them.

How wonderfully thoughtful!

I've decided to give these to others.

Do you have to?

You don't have to give me these.

If you don't want them, throw them away. I don't want to talk to you any more, Tuli, today at least. Please don't raise your voice. You've shouted enough in the morning.

Who's been tattling? Hem?

Yes. As long as you're in this house I warn you, you're not to speak a single harsh word to Hem. I pay Hem's salary, not your father. Hem brought up Brati. As long as she's here, it's up to you to be civil to her, but there'll be no rudeness, ever. It's Brati's birthday today, and you know she's been crying all day, and still you had to be nasty to her. Your behaviour was simply unforgivable.

Today! If you had such deep sentiments about today, how could you spend the whole day out?

You didn't heed my sentiments when you fixed the day. You chose the day because Tony's mother wished it. That I'm back home at all should be enough for you.

Neepa said, You could have thought of me, at least, Ma. I don't often come to spend a day with you.

Sujata smiled and said, How many days in the year do you think of me? You often drive down this road. Amit is out on tours most of the time, and you are always roaming around. Jyoti had typhoid, Suman had his birthday, you didn't have the time to come! I don't blame you, for that's how it happens. Then why should you expect me to sit at home and wait for you?

You . . .

Not a word more, Tuli. I've got to get ready.

Sujata went to her room and opened the wardrobe. Every nerve in her body screamed, No-no-no! But she had to go through the evening. It was an obligation. Her solitary cell. Sujata had let each one of them know that they could go their respective ways, but she would stick to her duties. She had sentenced herself to imprisonment. How could she break through the bars she herself had built? She chose a black-bordered Dhakai sari in white, with white flowers woven all over, and a white blouse.

She shut the wardrobe and entered the bathroom.

She shut the door behind her, let the shower run and sat down on the floor. It was cold, but she didn't feel it, because of the pain. The cold water soothed her. The water was ice cold. Ice. Slabs of ice. The blood stops flowing when a blood-stained, freshly killed corpse is laid on a slab of ice. Cold water. Cold. But no cold could match the cold of Brati's fingers, forehead, chest and hands. She had been with Brati all day today. His hands were so cold, ice cold, his eyelids, thick, black eyelashes shading his eyes half closed, the white of the skin tanned bronze, the hair dripping with ice water. Cold, cold, freezing, freezing, ice, ice, she had been with Brati all day. The night in the cremation ground. Brati under police escort. The floodlit crematorium. Its walls covered with scribbles. Name after name. Names, names, names, names. The aluminium door of the electric oven slammed shut. Brati. Brati was being roasted in the electric heat. She had been with Brati all day. Gather the ashes, pick up the navel, cover it with earth, it must be thrown into the Ganga. She had been with Brati all day.

She stopped the shower. Went on with the preparations mechanically. Her nerves, veins, heart, blood, screamed, No-no-no! She dried her body, her hair. Threw down the towel. Powdered her body. Put on her clothes. And tied her wet hair into a bun.

Brati used to ask, Ma, how can you go on doing your duty?

But that was how she had been trained from her childhood, to be eternally dutiful.

That was how she had been trained. And she kept herself under the strictest control. But now it feels as if everything, everything, has been such a waste. She had wasted herself. Has she been any good to anybody? Dibyanath? Neepa? Tuli? No one.

She opened the bathroom door and came out. She entered her room and stood before the mirror. Deep shadows under the eyes. Let them be. Under the near-blind eyes of Nandini were dark, dark shadows, like the perennial shadows upon the foothills of the mountains.

Sujata would never visit Nandini again, nor would she go to Somu's mother. Where would she go, then, searching for Brati? Or would she, too, stop searching for him some day?

After the funeral was over, Dibyanath had wept loudly before his other children, and said, Look at your mother. Her eyes are dry. Unnatural woman.

She had no tears to shed that day.

Was it possible that some day Sujata might be able to sit beside someone and cry, to utter Brati's name?

The very thought chilled her. A shudder passed through her. Was that when Brati would finally die? Was he not still alive, immured within her inconsolable grief? All was still not quiet, the prison walls rose higher, new watchtowers sprang up. Prison gates were not thrown open to receive prisoners. The vans approached the gates in the dark of night. Radio signals went off. Cranes swept down to pounce upon the prisoners with iron claws and haul them up to drop them within the prison compound. Calcutta wildly excited over *ashtami*, the second day of the Pujas.[20] Fire! A black car. Fire! An attempted escape. Fire! You can close the file on Habul Dutt now. Fire! File closed. A funeral procession under heavy police escort. Mourners following, faces grim with anger and determination. Young faces, all. How could Sujata give vent to her grief for Brati and reduce it to mere commonplace?

She wore a white shawl. Put on her slippers. Drank some water. A knock on the door. Bini looked in at the door.

Hair styled like Neepa's and Tuli's, the same sari and stole. They all wanted to be like each other. They never wanted to be themselves. And that is what passed for fashion.

Ma, are you ready?

Yes. What is Suman doing?

He's with his ayah. He'll go to bed now.

Come. Let's go downstairs.

Sujata switched off the lights. Came out of the room. Her nerves, sinews, heart, screamed No-no-no but she went down the stairs. To do what one hated to do was duty. Was there, somewhere inside her, a sense of pride at being so dutiful? Once, on the birthday of Neepa's daughter, Brati had told her that it was more important for her to visit the eye doctor.

Neepa will be disappointed.

No, Ma, she won't.

Sujata had kept silent.

Didi's disappointment is merely a matter of convention. But you know quite well, Ma, that her happiness or unhappiness does not depend in the least on what we do. Then why won't you go to the eye doctor?

Brati knew so much, he knew everything. And that is how he could reject everyone in the family so easily. Finally he had gone out. Then he came back. He said, Come, let's go to the eye doctor.

Will you come with me?

Yes. Come on, now.

Brati knew that it would be a strain for Sujata to go to the eye doctor with atropine in her eyes, so he had chosen to accompany her. On the way back he had dropped her off at Neepa's.

Won't you come in, Brati?

Brati had just smiled. Didn't say anything. He was wearing a dhoti and a shirt that day. He normally wore trousers, but was fond of wearing a dhoti once in a while. Even after he changed so completely, there were things he would think of which no one else would. After Brati was killed, Sujata came home late after going to Kantapukur.

She had gone with the hope that the police would hand over Brati's body to her as normal routine. But it was no shock to her when she learnt that they would not, that they would never give her the body. By then she was beyond being shocked by anything. She had come back. And then, on getting the news, had run there again. Thanks to Dibyanath's pleading and pulling strings, their post mortems had been done quickly. At that time the surgeon in the morgue would rub the naked corpse with formalin and carve the body open and stitch it up again—all at breakneck speed. He had to hurry. For there were vans speeding towards the morgue round the clock.

Sujata had come home towards noon. She would go to the cremation ground and wait for the dead Brati to arrive there. Back home she had found the members of the family silent, stunned, deeply disturbed over how to explain Brati's death to the others; suddenly, like Somu's mother, Hem had broken down in spontaneous grief, weeping unashamedly, knocking her head against the wall, lamenting, You were handed to me when you were only seven days old. They all said you wouldn't survive. Where have you left him today? She had said, There's no one any longer who'll care to bring me my gout medicine in the midst of a thousand worries of his own! Who will stop me in the street, when I'm bringing home the week's ration, and tell me— How can you walk with such a heavy load? Can't you take a rickshaw? He's no longer there to call a rickshaw for me and help me into it!

That night, after everything was over, who was it who, after Sujata returned, sat with Sujata's head in her lap? Hem, only Hem. Brati had been so concerned about Hem all the time. And yet Dibyanath would always describe him as an unfeeling son.

Sujata yearned to tell Brati—I can't bear to go down the stairs today, Brati. She longed to say—You would always tell me how difficult it was to be oneself. Brati, if only I could be myself today, and act as my heart dictated!

But if she had always followed the dictates of her heart, then Brati would not have been born at all. Fair, delicate, silken-haired, he had not shaved off his birth hair even when he had gone through the sacred thread ceremony. So the priest had been offered penance money. As a child, whenever he crossed the road, he would hold on to Sujata's finger firmly. That was Brati.

She shook her head. The drawing room was before her. A hubbub of talk and laughter. Did the earth belong only to the dead? The dead that ate, quarrelled and lived in a frenzy of lust and greed?

The dead that had lost all claim to respect? The dead that Brati refused to respect?

The dead that did not love? The dead that Brati therefore could not love?

Brati yearned to respect, to love and to be loved.

He still yearned for this, for all was not yet quiet. The times remained restless, disturbed, aggrieved, agonized, rebellious and turbulent.

Sujata pushed the curtain aside and entered the room.

Mrs Kapadia spoke of her guru. At some distance, Neepa, with a Scotch[21] in her hand, played at hide and seek, giggling, while Balai Dutt, her husband's cousin, chased her with a piece of meat on a fork, trying to put it into her mouth.

Nargis, Tony's sister, in skintight top and trousers of saffron-coloured nylon wool, was dancing and talking to someone over her shoulder. Nargis was a devotee of the guru. She had resolved to preach the Swami's teachings throughout India. She held a glass of lemon cordial in one hand. A confirmed dypsomaniac, she was confined to a nursing home, and came out only on special occasions. But she never forgot to wear the holy colour, saffron.

Bini was nowhere to be seen. Tuli, at the centre of a group made up of Amit, Neepa's husband, Tony and Tony's friends, broke into loud laughter. Then she inclined her cheek. Tony gave her a kiss. A camera bulb flashed.

Mrs Kapadia held a tall Scotch in her hand. Sujata was part of the group that listened to her. Sujata's lips were slightly parted in a polite smile. Her brain was not responding. Her body was tired.

When I saw the Swami, my dear, you won't believe it, but something in me caught fire. Then I saw the halo behind the Swami's head. Like a lamp burning. The light grew brighter and brighter and burned like a thousand suns.

They had taken Kush to the rubber-tubed room, strapped and immobile. Two thousand-watt lamps blazed right onto his face, burned and burned. All the nails from his fingers had been plucked out. Then they pierced each nerve centre of the body with needles. At a stretch for forty-eight hours, then for seventy-two hours, then they had said, You are free. He was taken out and brought home. Then they flung him down in front of his house, and shot him. His eyeballs had melted with the heat.

But Mrs Kapadia's vision had not been damaged in the light of a thousand suns. She had only discovered an inner vision.

The Swami was flying his own plane. He just looked at me, and said, Come to me. Meet me at Miami. Think of that, dear, how could he guess that I was going to Miami? He said, You are the girl in the book you are carrying. Do you know which book it was, dear? Black girl in Search of God. I was black, dear. My soul was black. I found my God. And all was light! In both the senses, luminous and weightless.

Something was dead within Nandini. One grows heavy after death. How heavy Brati's hand had become. Dead feelings, too, perhaps, grow as heavy as a dead body. Did Nandini drag her feet under the dead weight of the dead emotions within her? She would never become a normal woman again, never a wife or a mother. Those who had loved so fiercely the streetlights, human beings, each particle of dust, were denied motherhood for ever. Women who could not suffer a child's company, who roamed from one man to another, one glass of liquor to another, laughing, they were chosen to bring children into the earth, into a life devoid of love and affection. What a waste!

And the Swami was my guru from that very moment. Not only mine. Some day everyone in the whole world will be his disciple. Like Vivekananda. America has discovered him, as she had once discovered Vivekananda. Now India will know him.

Jishu Mitter was gaping at Mrs Kapadia. He pleaded with Sujata, Please introduce me to her. Just do it, please. I'm dying to know her. Please.

Mrs Kapadia, meet Jishu Mitter, our friend.

So pleased!

Molly Mitter, Jishu's wife, whispered to Sujata, She thinks that you don't know English. So she's speaking in Bengali for your benefit. How funny! Have you noticed what she's wearing? Insufferable bitch! Showing off her diamonds! To me!

Mrs Kapadia caught the word 'diamonds'. She turned a pair of smiling, glittering eyes on Molly, to say, Diamonds are a must. The Swami says the diamond is a symbol of the soul. Purity.

How nice!

But I haven't forgiven you, my dear.

Why?

You didn't let my Golden Retriever win the prize in the dogshow.

Not me. It was my Rover.

Yes. I was so angry. But when I saw your dog!

She turned to Sujata and said, You won't believe me, dear, but something in me went mad with envy.

Jishu Mitter said, Tell us about the Swami.

He is God himself. He is the Almighty. He wants India to have this poverty, so that it knows suffering. When He wills, everyone will be rich.

Really?

Of course. When I told him about Tony and Tuli's marriage, he went into meditation. At the end of it he said, the girl is very, very unhappy. There's an evil shadow lying over their house.

He said that?

Yes. He promised to give them a few flowers when they went to the States. They should plant the flowers around their house.

Molly Mitter suddenly turned to Sujata and said, How can you convert, Sujata? Don't you have your own guru?

Convert?

Well, it was Mr Chatterjee who told us that the whole family would be converted to the Swami's faith.

I don't know anything about it.

If you have a guru already, can you change your guru?

I don't have a guru, Molly.

But didn't Ronu and Brati once go to see your guru, when they were in school? To find out how they'd fare in the examinations?

He was my mother-in-law's priest. She used to have horoscopes drawn up by him.

Lakshmishwar Mishra. He had drawn up Brati's horoscope too. Sujata had studied the horoscope numberless times—long life, nobody could kill him, no threat of disease or injury . . . Sujata had torn up the horoscope.

Molly Mitter said to Mrs Kapadia, You know, her younger son Brati . . .

Sujata said to Mrs Kapadia, Excuse me, Mrs Kapadia, I'll be back in a minute . . .

Mrs Kapadia felt soft after three tall whiskies. She raised her handkerchief to her eyes.

I know! Oh dear! How you must be suffering. You must let me tell you, dear, what the Swami has said.

Oh, certainly.

Sujata moved away.

Jishu Mitter said, It's his death anniversary today.

Is that so?

Molly Mitter said, That boy Brati, I never trusted him. Do you know what he said the day he left? He said that he would be spending the night with Ronu. And he had had no contact with Ronu since their first year at college. I'll be staying with Ronu! As if he could be Ronu's friend. There was nothing in the newspapers the next day. I mean Brati's name wasn't there. Jishu went to his club. What a blessing our area was free. We could go to the club every day. Otherwise how could we have survived? I didn't look into the newspapers those days. I didn't let anybody read the newspapers. What horrifying news they carried. Jishu quickly came back from the club and told me, Chatterjee's son has been killed.

How unnerving for you!

Then my elder brother—yes, the DC[22]—rang me up to ask whether Brati had come to our place. Jishu at once packed Ronu off to Bombay.

You did right!

We naturally came to offer our condolences. Chatterjee had a bad time. How hard he worked to hush things up! We felt for him. As you know, Sujata is a thoroughly unfeeling wife. She spoilt her son. Otherwise how could someone from a family like this . . . ?

Jishu Mitter said, What awful days those were. Where were you then?

In the States.

Tony?

He was here. As Molly said, Park Street, Camac Street, and a few such areas were free.[23] Saroj Pal, Tony's friend, was the Operation-in-Charge. Brilliant boy! What courage! The way he caught them.

Really?

Molly Mitter said, What foolishness! You kill the gems of society. And what do you gain out of that? You get killed yourselves. And in the process all the honest traders had to run away from the state with their capital.

Telling me? I flew to Bombay from the States.

They wouldn't let me come to Calcutta from Bombay.

They told us, they were killing off all the rich people in Calcutta. Do you know what I did?

What did you do?

Mrs Kapadia's face glowed with pride. She said, I put on a cotton sari, and travelled by train—second class—to Calcutta. I said, my husband and my son need me. I have Swami's blessings, no force in the world can kill me.

Jishu Mitter drew this story to a close—But you have to admit that Sujata looks lovely! In white. Grief. Wonderful.

Molly Mitter said, That's a stunt. Sujata knew everyone would be wearing colours this evening. As a contrast, she chose to wear white.

Mrs Kapadia asked her, Can you tell me what make-up she's using, dear? Something unusual.

Make-up? Sujata? Dear Mrs Kapadia, she never does.

But why? She's beautiful.

Tony said, Let me introduce my beautiful mother-in-law. Ma, he's a journalist. He's been dying to meet you.

Tony spoke in Bengali. He had grown up in Calcutta. He spoke Bengali well.

The journalist said, Wonderful party. Your daughter's wearing a beautiful sari. Mr Chatterjee speaks excellent Sanskrit. You have a typical Bengali home.

Have you had anything to eat?

A lot. By the way, may I interview you?

Me?

I write for a women's journal from Bombay. You are a mother, a wife, and a bank officer. That you can combine a home and a career . . .

I'm not an officer.

But Tony said . . .

I began as a clerk. In twenty years, I have moved up to be a Section-in-Charge.

How nice.

Therefore . . .

Well, your son was killed. From the angle of a sorrowing mother . . .

No. Pardon me.

Sujata moved away at once. Her photograph in a women's magazine! 'A Bereaved Mother Speaks'. They just won't let Brati be with her. Yet the whole day she had been with Brati. See . . . My son was . . . The fashionable ladies of Bombay, wives of those who owned racing horses, industrialists, the film stars, all of them reading about Sujata and Brati.

Sujata walked up to Amit.

Amit, have you had anything to eat?

Yes, Ma.

Have you checked if your friends have . . . ?

They've all eaten. There was whisky being served, and yet her son-in-law stood sober. Sujata was surprised. Dibyanath had chosen Amit. Neepa had run off with the young man who was teaching her to play the sitar. Dibyanath had traced her, brought her back, and married her off to Amit within a month. He had spent a fortune. Amit was weak-spirited, cowardly, a high-up executive, and the pampered son of a rich father. Neepa's husband.

Sujata felt sorry for Amit. There was a time when he did not drink at all. But now he drank to get drunk.

Amit began drinking after Neepa began to live with his cousin in his house.

Sujata never knew why Amit could not tell his cousin off, or talk it out with his wife. That is what people would normally do under such circumstances. Before the situation got out of control, he could have tried to talk it over with his cousin.

He could have turned his cousin out of his house.

He could have asked his wife to leave his house. He could have taken recourse to the law, to the courts.

But Amit did nothing. He only drank. Because Dibyanath maintained the custom, Amit and Neepa paid an annual visit on the day sons-in-law were entertained.[24] They went to pay homage together once a year to Amit's guru. Amit slept on the second floor. Their daughter and her nurse shared a room on the first floor; Balai and Neepa had their bedrooms side by side on the same floor.

It was all like a festering, malignant cancer. The dead pretended to live within relationships that were long dead and thus keep up a masquerade of life. Sujata felt that if she went close enough to Amit, Neepa and Balai, the stench of carrion would overwhelm her. They were contaminated and diseased from the very womb. The society that Brati and his comrades had tried to exterminate kept thousands starving in order to nourish and support these vermin. It was a society that gave the dead the right to live, and denied it to the living. But what was Balai saying?

Where are they all now? They have all taken to their heels, they keep away from their old localities. *Arre baba*, didn't Dhiman write all those soppy lyrics over Baranagar? But crying is not enough. They had to cut down more than a hundred in order to bring peace to Baranagar. What tension till they were ripped to pieces!

Which Dhiman was he talking about? Dhiman Roy? The same Dhiman that Nandini had mentioned? Sujata saw an extremely fair young girl in a maxi made out of a shawl, glass in hand, place a hand on his shoulder. She said,

Isn't their poetry just fantastic?

Balai said, Dhiman whines over the twenty thousand young men languishing in the prisons. But don't you see the fun? When the action–counteraction was on, they were all whining over the tragedy of Bangladesh in the newspapers. Now that things are under control, he feels he is safe enough to write.

Don't be unfair. How he writes! His last poem brought tears to my eyes. Here he is. We were talking about your poetry. When do you write? You are so busy. Really, you are truly committed to the cause.

Dhiman Roy, in his forties, unattractive and blunt-featured. He went through an actor's swift change of face to don a mask of humility. In his heavy, grating voice, he said, Can a poet write about anything else?

Really—when I read the poem! Anup Datta, you know him, Anup said, he feels!

Everyone today thinks about them!

Dhiman Roy bit into a lump of butter almost artistically and sipped his whisky. Sujata had heard that one did not get drunk if one ate enough butter. She watched Dhiman and knew that he was determined not to get drunk.

I know that, said Neepa suddenly. Neepa had had a lot of whisky. There was defiance writ large across her face.

Oh, do you?—mocked Amit.

Sure. That washed-out poet who lifts ideas from others, what experience does he have to boast of? My brother died. What was your sympathetic poet doing then? Hiding behind whose skirts? Haven't I heard all about it from Balai?

As far as I remember you were in the soup yourself over Brati. You were ashamed of your brother.

Who told you?

I'm telling you.

You were warning me all the time.

Not me.

Liar.

Take that back.

I won't.

I'm one of the Gangulys of Khidirpur, one of the oldest families of the city. I'm not going to take something like that from a three-paisa whore like you . . .

Amit!

Sujata warned him in a low voice.

A few unpleasant, explosive moments. The wick burned and burned and burned, edging closer and closer to the gunpowder. But the burning wick stopped short of the gunpowder, when Neepa suddenly broke into a ripple of laughter.

Ma, you don't understand a thing. Don't you see how we enjoy these fights?

Have your fights in your own home.

Sujata moved away. The party was warming up. The tempo was rising. They were now all drunk. Tony's sister,

Nargis, was banging two ashtrays together, dancing, chanting Swami! Swami! Jishu Mitter squatted on his haunches, clapping and swaying slightly.

Amit sounded annoyed—Your mother is a real spoil-sport.

He now decided to get totally drunk. He poured whisky into his glass, without a drop of water, and gulped it down.

Balai said, Neepa, let's go.

Let's go.

Let's go to Sarat's. There's a film session today. He's showing a fresh lot brought from Paris.

Balai clicked his tongue between his lips and his cheeks, and made a strange sound. Naked and meaty. The sound suggested the kind of film it would be. It was bound to be exciting.

Let's go.

They went out.

Dhiman Roy said to Amit, You're a strange person!

Why?

Didn't you notice your wife going off with Balai to see films?

What's that to you?

Balai! Even a calendar could . . .

Arre baba! You cultivate the rich so you can get your free liquor. You're getting it free, lap it up! Why do you rack your brains over other things?

But with Balai . . .

Amit sniggered like a cunning fox. He said, I know Balai. He's my cousin.

Cousin?

Yes, sir. We both claim descent from Mahimaranjan Ganguly, both grandsons, one from his son, the other from his daughter.

I see.

Do you believe in fate?

Of course not. I don't believe in god, I don't believe in fate.

Crap.

What did you say?

Rubbish. Why should an atheist like you visit my office twice a day?

You are drunk.

You aren't. You have to accept fate, sir, fate.

Why?

What else can it be but fate? Has Balai left any young woman in the family untouched, let alone my wife? He began with my aunt, that is, his aunt too. Why should he let Neepa alone? Still, Balai has a sense of class. He never plays his games outside the family circle.

Your wife with Balai . . .

Balai's my cousin, and a friend too. Do you know his connections? If you come in his way . . .

Sir, you're a real liberal.

Truly liberal . . .

Mr Kapadia said, I'm truly liberal.

Dibyanath said, I know.

Mr Kapadia placed a finger on one of the black buttons of his impeccable suit, as he said, All the problems of the country will come to an end if you follow my policy.

How?

Mr Kapadia spoke in flawless Bengali—What's the country's problem? We cannot accomplish integration. The country is breaking into pieces under the pressure of so many religions, races and languages. Food is no problem. Do you see food riots anywhere? The peasants are very well off. They are all buying radio sets. Employment? Lots of people are getting new jobs. National wealth? Everyone has money. Otherwise how come new houses are coming up, people are buying cars and eating expensively?

True.

How can language be a problem? Learn the language of the place you are in. I sell liquor in this part of the country, so I've learnt Bengali.

You've mastered it.

One has to. It's Tagore's language.

True.

So that's how I solve the language problem. Religion? You don't need all those religions. Burn down all the temples, all the mosques, everything. Follow the Swami. The Swami is God Incarnate. Follow him.

That's it.

We, the Swami's children in India, have opened offices in Delhi, Bombay, Calcutta and Madras. We'll provide jobs for six thousand people. We've bought aeroplanes and helicopters. We'll print the Swami's message in all the Indian languages. We'll spread his message all over the country from the sky above. In no time they will all follow the Swami.

True.

So that takes care of religion. Races, communities? Make a law that nobody will be allowed to marry within one's state, one's race or one's language. A Bengali marries a Punjabi, an Oriya marries a Bihari, an Assamese marries a Marathi, and the problem is solved.

Like Tony and Tuli . . .

I'm grateful for this.

What a thing to say. I'm grateful. Proud.

Me, too.

Getting to be related to the Great Moghul of the wine trade . . .

Why do you underestimate yourself?

Tony is a great boy.

Tuli is a great girl.

Jackie is a great son.

So is Jyoti.

Nargis is a great girl.

Neepa too.

You have a great family.

So have you.

Your pedigree . . .

You are zamindars.

We are kulins.[25]

Kulins? That is great.

I'll show you my family tree some day.

That'll be great.

Yes, I'll show it to you—

I had something to ask you, Chatterjee . . .

What?

Mrs Chatterjee hasn't been able to get over the shock of your younger son's . . .

Oh no, she's all right.

How could your son . . .

Misguided.

Must have been.

Bad company. Bad friends.

Must be that.

Do you know how close we were, father and son?

Tuli told us.

Like babies. We had no secrets from each other.

That's how it should be.

He respected me like God himself.

With such a father, he had to.

And when that son . . .

Ohh!

He broke my heart.

That's only natural.

The shock I had . . .

Don't grieve. The Swami says, there's no such thing as death. It's just your body that dies, and then your souls will meet in heaven, and you'll find your son just the way he was in life.

Did the Swami say 'I'll see him'?

Oh, yes.

I'll follow the Swami.

You should.

This is my wife. Did you hear the beautiful things he was saying, dear? Why don't you join us and listen?

I heard everything. I was sitting right behind you.

Mrs Chatterjee, whisky?

Thanks. I don't drink.

Are you feeling unwell?

No.

Sujata moved away. Bini was calling her. The pain racked her again and again. Waves of pain. Like waves breaking. Everything seemed to be spinning, fading away, returning to clarity. Jyoti must have put on a record. A frenzied jazz.

What is it, Bini?

Ma, Tuli is calling you.

Why?

A special friend of Tony's is here.

Where's he?

Outside.

Why outside?

He won't get down from the car.

Ask him to get down.

Ma, did you stumble?

It's the pain again.

Why don't you sit down?

No.

Let me call him in.

No. I'll go myself.

Why do you have to go? Let me go.

Tuli will raise a row.

Then let's go.

Let me ask him to get down. You bring a box of sweets with you. If he doesn't get down, we can give him the packet at least.

That's better.

As the pain grew, it was less cold, it felt warm.

Sujata laid the shawl aside. She stepped out.

Cold. Winter. The North Wind. The dark garden. Darkness. If she could get lost in this darkness? If she never had to enter that room again? The black car stood on the street before the gate.

Black car. Black van. Steel net on the windows, over the rear door. Helmeted heads behind the net. Who sits in the front? Next to the driver? The engine hummed, it was running.

Dressed in spotless white. Brass badge. DCDD[26] Saroj Pal. A brave son of Mother Bengal, Saroj Pal the lion-hearted. The aluminium door bearing the slogan—No Mercy for Saroj Pal—slammed shut with a clang. Brati within. Lying cold and dead.

Saroj Pal.

Yes, I have a mother.

No, your son didn't go to Digha.

No, we won't let you keep these.

No, you won't get the photographs.

You failed to teach your son properly.

Your son had ganged up with antisocials.

Your son deserved no mercy.

You should have found out what your son was doing, and you should have asked him to surrender to us.

No, you won't get the body.

No, you won't get the body.

No, you won't get the body.

Sujata looked at him. Saroj Pal looked at her. Mother of 1084. Mother of Brati Chatterjee. Because he knew he would have to face her, he hadn't wanted to come.

Bini came forward.

Won't you get down?

No.

Not even for a minute?

No. I'm on duty. Give my best wishes to Tony and Tuli.

Take the packet of sweets, please.

Thanks. I'm in a rush. Goodbye.

Start. The car roared and left.

Duty still? Still in uniform? The black car, the bullet-proof chain armour beneath the shirt, the pistol in the holster, the helmeted sentry in the rear seat?

Where's the unquiet? Where's the duty? In Bhowa-nipur, in Ballygunge, in Gariahat, in Garia, in Behala, in Barasat, in Baranagar, in Baghbazar? Where's the duty?

Where will the shop shutters slam shut, the house doors close, pedestrians, cycles, street dogs and rickshaws scatter in panic?

Where will the sirens blare? The streets resound to the clamp clamp clamp of boots, the roaring of vans, the rat-a-tat-tat of shots?

Where will Brati run to? Again? Where will Brati run to? To what land that knew no killers, no shots, no vans, no jails?

This city—the Gangetic plains of Bengal—the forests and hills of north Bengal—the snowy regions further up—the rocks, the dry beds and dams of central Bengal—the salt water forests of the Sundarbans—the paddy fields, the factories—the tea plantations, the coalfields—where will you run to, Brati? Where will you lose yourself again? Don't run away, Brati. Come to me, Brati, come back. Don't run any more.

Sujata had found him again after searching all day, he was in the midst of everything, he was everywhere. But if the vans sped out again and the threatening sirens pierced the sky, Brati would be lost again. Come back home, Brati, come back home. Don't run any more. Come back to your mother, Brati. Don't run like this, Brati. They won't let you go, Brati, they'll drag you out from wherever you hide. Come to me, Brati.

Ma! You're falling down!

Sujata pushed Bini away. She came running back. She stood at the door to the room.

Everything rocked and swayed and spun. As if someone was making the cadavers dance. Putrefying cadavers, all of them—Dhiman, Amit, Dibyanath, Mr Kapadia, Tuli, Tony, Jishu Mitter, Molly Mitter, Mrs Kapadia—

Did Brati die so that these corpses with their putrefied lives could enjoy all the images of all the poetry of the world, the red rose, the green grass, the neon lights, the smiles of mothers, the cries of children—for ever? Did he die for this? To leave the world to these corpses?

Never.

Brati . . .

Sujata's long-drawn-out, heart-rending, poignant cry burst, exploded like a massive question, spread through all the houses of the city, crept underneath the city, rose to the sky. The winds carried it from one end of the state to the other, from one corner of the earth to another, to the dark piles and pillars that stood witness to history, and beyond history into the foundations of faith that underlie the scriptures. The cry set oblivion itself, the present and the future atremble, reeling under its impact. All the contentment in every happy existence cracked to pieces.

It was a cry that smelt of blood, protest, grief.

Then everything went dark. Sujata's body fell to the ground.

Dibyanath screamed, The appendix has burst!

1 A worker, traditionally of low/'untouchable' caste, who is usually given the most unpleasant jobs, for example, carrying dead bodies and removing dead and decaying flesh, working in cremation grounds.

2 Officer-in-Charge.

3 A low-grade employee. The term is roughly equivalent to 'waiter'.

4 Literally, 'Call God's name!'; cried aloud by those who accompany a Bengali Hindu funerary procession.

5 A book of poems for and about children by Rabindranath Tagore.

6 Good deeds and meditation.

7 Prayer room.

8 Calcutta Metropolitan Development Authority.

9 Elder sister.

10 Neighbourhood youth club for boys of the locality.

11 Elder brother's wife.

12 Elder brother.

13 Brahman initiatory rite in which a boy, for the first time, dons the sacred thread denoting his caste.

14 Elder sister, but not the eldest (who would be Bor-di).

15 Here referring to white tourists, usually low-budget travellers.

16 Vermilion applied in the parting of a woman's hair is a sign of marriage.

17 Somu's full name.

18 Mother's sister; also a form of address for an older woman.

19 Father's mother.

20 The Durga Puja festival is Calcutta's major annual festival, which the whole city celebrates for four days, leading up to the immersion of the Durga idol in the Hoogly river on the final (*dashami*) day.

21 Scotch whisky. At a time when foreign liquor was only available on the black market at exorbitant rates, it was a status symbol to serve it at parties.

22 Deputy Commissioner.

23 Park Street and Camac Street are both in central Calcutta, a predominantly upper-class and westernized area of the city when compared to the neighbourhoods mentioned elsewhere in the text.

24 *Jamaishashthi* is a Bengali custom, a day on which in-laws honour their sons-in-law.

25 Member of a family of a high social class which enjoyed ritual status.

26 Deputy Commissioner, Detective Department.